Honey, We Missed Our Honeymoon

A Romantic Comedy Novel

ANGIE PEPPER

Chapter 1

Malorie Meyers sat alone in her rented room, gazing longingly out the window. The rain that had been pouring down for five days had finally cleared, and people were out enjoying the sun in groups of two, three, four, five, and more. There wasn't a single person walking solo on the busy sidewalk below the quaint bed-and-breakfast.

Lonely people knew better than to subject others to their loneliness. They stayed holed up in their rooms, where they belonged, with the television on and three abandoned paperbacks on the bedside table.

It was a good thing that Malorie would be flying back home tomorrow. At home, the kids who worked at the coffee shop had learned how to spell Malorie's name. That was basically the same as having friends. Also, back home in the city, she didn't have to answer pesky questions about why she was all alone in the honeymoon suite at the extremely romantic Half-Moon B and B.

Malorie tore her gaze away from the window and surveyed the room. The bed, covered in sumptuous red linens, beckoned her to sleep. She could slumber until this terrible idea of a vacation could finally end. Great idea, but it was only two o'clock. Even with the prescription pills her doctor had provided the week before, she wouldn't be able to sleep straight through until checkout time.

Malorie checked her phone for the one millionth time.

There were no new messages from Lars.

She sent him a text: *You should see this room! Wish you were here.*

She didn't send a photo of herself wrapped in the red silky sheets. Malorie did have *some* dignity. Plus she had already sent one the day before, to no response.

There was a scratch at the door.

"Just a sec," she called out, frantically removing her wrinkled and food-stained shirt. She replaced it with another shirt that was merely wrinkled.

Malorie opened the door to find her new buddy, a Basset Hound named Bingo, staring up at her with his adorable saggy face. Standing behind Bingo was the human known as Albert, one of the owners of Half-Moon B and B.

Albert, a flamboyant man of sixty-two, said, "Bingo needs to get outside for some fresh air. And so do you, honey." He handed Malorie the leash. "The sun is shining. I know your stay here didn't work out the way you'd hoped, but you are not going to waste your last day with us. When people stay at the Half-Moon B and B, a good time is guaranteed. Do *not* make me force you to have a good time."

Malorie accepted the leash. "I guess I can take Bingo for a walk," she said, her voice monotone.

"He'd better come back smiling," Albert said.

They both looked down at the saggy-jowled Basset Hound.

Malorie asked, "How would you be able to tell?"

"Basset Hounds can smile," Albert said. "When they do, it lights up the whole universe. You should try it sometime, honey." He grabbed Malorie by the shoulders and firmly rolled back her slumping shoulders. "Stand up straight. You'll feel better instantly. And when you get outside, try looking at something besides the sidewalk. Look up and around. Don't waste money or time. People come from all over the country to enjoy our small-town charm.

You *will* enjoy our small-town charm today, and you *will* report back to me at dinner."

She asked, "What's for dinner?"

He ignored her question as he knelt by the dog and rubbed Bingo's long, velvet ears. "You make sure Malorie has a good time today," he said in the who's-a-good-boy voice he used for his dog. "If she lets out one of her big, heavy sighs, bite her." He pointed at Malorie's ankles. "Bite her on the ankles."

"Fine," Malorie said. "I'll take Bingo for a quick jaunt, and I'll keep my chin up."

"No sighing," Albert said. "And don't you dare make it quick. You are banned from this establishment for a minimum of two hours. It's a new policy."

"There's a new policy that says I have to leave for two hours?"

"We have to do something important with your room," he said. "We have to flip the mattress."

"Right now?"

"Who's the innkeeper here? It's me. I know about flipping mattresses." He pulled two bags from his pockets. One contained dog treats and the other was empty. "These are all Bingo needs until dinner. Now you have no excuses." He pointed toward the stairwell. "Get going."

Malorie fought back the urge to cry at the kindness of Albert's tough love.

She pulled on a pair of sandals, and she reluctantly left the safety of her room. On the way outside, she listened to Albert's instructions about the best route to the beach and Bingo's favorite locations for sniffing. She only caught about half of what Albert was saying. Her mind had been so muddled these past few days. A two-hour walk with the dog wasn't going to change anything, she thought, but she would do it if only to repay the kindness that Albert and his partner had shown her.

Albert gave her one last command, "Get ice cream," he said.

"How much do you need me to pick up?"

"Not for us," he said. "For yourself. Get a double scoop, and don't forget to flirt with Shawn."

"Shawn?" Malorie pretended to not know who that was. She hadn't been out of her room much, but she had been to the ice cream shop, and she had met Shawn. She hugged herself and rubbed her arm, nervous about the idea of talking to Shawn, let alone flirting with him.

Albert narrowed his eyes. "Honey, you know *exactly* who I'm talking about," he said. "Now go. Your two-hour banishment starts now."

Malorie said, "Good luck flipping all the mattresses."

Albert blew a kiss to Bingo, told him to be a good boy for Malorie, then shooed her away.

Chapter 2

Albert wasn't wrong about the appeal of the small, seaside town. It was a fairytale setting full of antique shops, cafes, artist studios, and other quaint places perfect for wasting time.

Malorie Meyers could see it was the sort of place people liked. And those people were all around her, strolling the boardwalk with a romantic partner, family, or friends. The only single person she saw on her outing was a man feeding the birds, and he was quickly joined by a similar man who gave him a jovial greeting.

She took a seat on a bench overlooking the water. Bingo wanted up on the bench, too, so she hoisted up the short-legged dog to sit next to her. She was rewarded by several wet slurps on her arm.

"Is that a smile, Bingo? Do you like sitting on the bench like a person?"

Bingo gave her his usual Basset Hound expression. The universe wasn't lighting up, so it couldn't have been a smile.

She offered him the treat that Albert had sent, and then he gave her what might have been a smile. It was hard to tell.

"We are having a good time," she told the dog. "If anyone asks, that's what you tell them."

Bingo settled with his chin on his paws. Then he lifted his nose to the air, sniffed, and turned around to face the opposite direction. He smacked his lips. Malorie followed the dog's gaze to Treat-o-Rama, the ice cream and candy shop.

"I'm not going to get ice cream," Malorie said. "Just because Albert told me to doesn't mean anything. He's not the boss of me. And you won't tell on me, will you, Bingo?"

Bingo smacked his lips and let out a sad A-WOOO.

"Shush," she said. "People are looking."

Nobody was looking.

Bingo howled again, louder and longer.

"Tattletale," she said, letting out an extra-long sad sigh.

Bingo gave her a look that said he didn't *want to* bite her ankles, but he knew his marching orders, and he would at least drool on her ankles if she kept sighing like that.

"Fine," she said. "You win."

She helped the dog hop down, and they headed toward Treat-o-Rama.

Like most food establishments, the shop didn't allow pets, so she left Bingo tied to the pet station in front. There was a bucket of water, and Bingo seemed happy enough.

Treat-o-Rama had a vintage 1950s decor, with a bright checkerboard floor and gleaming chrome everywhere. They sold candy and other novelties, but most people went there for the ice cream. It was made locally, with supplies from nearby farms. The cooler held sixteen flavors, and Malorie had sampled —using the tiny sample spoons—fifteen of the flavors over the past five days. She didn't like the look of the black licorice.

The shop was family run, and the young man who worked in the afternoons was named Shawn, according to his name tag. Malorie had stared at his name tag a lot, because looking directly at Shawn's utterly gorgeous face made her eyes hurt.

Shawn had light-blue eyes that contrasted with dark, thick, lush eyelashes. His hair was coffee brown, straight, and shiny. His eyebrows were thick and unruly, on a prominent brow. He had hollow cheeks and a square jaw. He was average height, with an athletic build. His white apron was tied tightly around a waist that seemed far too narrow for a person who worked at an ice cream shop.

He looked like the model Treat-o-Rama might hire to pose in a photograph for their advertising, not a man who would actually be found there, handing out samples and making replacement cones for crying kids who'd just dropped one on the sidewalk.

He was young, too. Early twenties, if that. He had the eager-puppy-dog look that the guys who were Malorie's age, thirty-something, didn't have. Guys her age were always looking out of the sides of their eyes, always scanning. This guy, Shawn, looked directly at people, as though whoever he was talking to at the moment was the only person that existed. And that was exactly why Malorie had to stare at Shawn's name tag instead of his light-blue eyes.

The interior of the shop was quiet except for the hum of the coolers and the Elvis song playing on the vintage jukebox.

As Malorie approached the counter, her breath caught in her throat, and her heart began to race.

Shawn hadn't seen her yet. He stood behind the counter, fastidiously wiping down surfaces with his lean, muscular arms. She wondered what sports he played. Volleyball for sure, she guessed. It was popular with the young people who hung around the beach. She imagined he would be heading out to join a group of equally good-looking twenty-somethings after his shift at the Treat-o-Rama.

"Just a moment," Shawn said without looking up.

"I'm in no hurry."

He immediately dropped the cloth in a sink and looked up. A big smile spread across his face when he saw it was Malorie. His light-blue eyes twinkled as he brushed the tousled coffee-brown hair off his forehead.

"You're getting to be a regular," he said. "You might have to move here permanently so you can keep coming to see me."

"I'll talk to the-powers-that-be at my job about opening a branch down here."

He hooked his thumb into the tie of his apron and gazed at her. "Some sort of designer clothing place, right? That's where you work?"

"You remembered. Yes. We make sportswear and loungewear. It's not exactly high fashion, but it pays the bills, and people always need sweatpants. I'm wearing some of our line right now."

His gaze swept over her body, down her wrinkled T-shirt and stretchy pants, moving slowly, as though taking in a spectacular, hand-sequined evening gown.

Heaven help her, but the way he looked at Malorie made her wish she was wearing an evening gown.

"It's just loungewear," she said, trying to pull the shirt straight. "It looks better when it's not wrinkled. This fabric doesn't do well in a suitcase. I'm going to let our textiles buyer know."

"Those aren't suitcase wrinkles," Shawn said, his light-blue eyes twinkling as he teased her.

"Busted," she said. "I'm a lazy slob. You got me."

"I don't think you are," he said. "Sounds to me like you have a pretty busy career back home, and, just between us," he leaned forward, resting his tanned, gorgeous elbows on the counter, "the Half-Moon isn't where the lazy slobs stay when they're in town."

"You would know," she said lightly. "Sounds to me like you're the expert on things in this town."

"I know a few things." He made his eyebrows rise up twice suggestively. "Since you haven't taken off yet, maybe I could show you a few of the sights."

"I'm not interested in the tourist-trap stuff. I don't need to get a picture of myself with my face in one of those wooden cut-outs. No offense."

"None taken. I wouldn't dream of taking you there. I'm talking about the fun stuff the locals do. You'll have to sign an agreement that you won't tell the other city people back home about it, though. We don't want our secret spots to get overrun by outsiders."

She tilted her head back as her throat made an unfamiliar sound. It must have been a laugh.

Malorie's body flushed with heat. Was she flirting with Shawn? Was this considered flirting? She might know if she'd spent any time at all in the last decade dating someone other than Lars.

Shawn said, "I'm off work at seven. You should come by if you're feeling adventurous."

"I, uh..."

"You can wear sweatpants if you want," he said. "We don't dress up fancy around here."

Malorie was trying to think of an excuse when a woman came into the shop in a flurry, the hard heels of her shoes cracking angrily on the checkerboard floor.

Shawn took a couple steps back, his hands rising protectively to his chest. "Sharise!"

The woman—Sharise—stepped right up to the counter, shoving in front of Malorie as though she wasn't even there.

"You can't hide from me, *Shawn*," the woman said, speaking his name as though it was a dirty word. "I know where you live and I know where you work, *Shawn*."

Shawn said, "Sharise, I'm helping a customer right now."

"It can wait," Sharise said, not even looking at Malorie. "Your stupid ice cream isn't going anywhere."

Shawn waved over Sharise's shoulder at Malorie and said, "Please wait, miss. There's a lemon cream you need to try. We swapped it out for the black licorice."

If Shawn had called her ma'am instead of miss, Malorie would have left right then. But he hadn't. She felt flattered and attractive in spite of her wrinkled appearance.

Sharise started in on something in a hushed tone too low for Malorie to hear. Sharise sounded like an angry hive of bees.

Malorie wandered over to the wooden counter along the front window. She picked up the local newspaper. The front-page news item was about a busted water main. Malorie pretended to read about the water main.

A dog barked. It wasn't the deep, rumbly bark of a Basset Hound. Bingo, waiting obediently on the sidewalk, shot Malorie a look through the window as if to say he was curious, too.

There was another sharp bark. It was coming from inside the ice cream shop. It was coming from inside Sharise's purse. A caramel-brown Chihuahua with big eyes and a pink collar was glancing around nervously. The dog made eye contact with Malorie and started struggling to get out of the purse.

Sharise let out an angry huff and dropped the purse on the floor so the dog could climb out. The pooch ran over to Malorie, wagging her tiny Chihuahua tail excitedly.

Malorie knelt down and checked the name on the pink collar. "Hello there, Princess."

Princess put her little front paws on Malorie's knee and licked her chin.

Sharise turned around and said sharply, "Stop it!"

Malorie startled and pulled away from the dog.

Sharise said to the Chihuahua, "Princess, don't lick strangers. We don't know where they've been."

Shawn said, "That's not very nice." To Malorie, he said, "I'm sorry, miss. You can pet Princess. She's a good girl." He said to Sharise angrily, "And she's my dog. You need to give her back."

"You're so selfish!" Sharise went from a low, angry-hive-of-bees tone to a loud, hysterical one. "You're so selfish, and you do stupid things. You know, Eric never treated me like this. He didn't take me for granted!"

"Let's not bring Eric into this. Now try to stay calm. Do you want an ice cream? My treat."

"Don't play cute with me," Sharise said angrily. "I don't want free ice cream. You're trying to make me fat so I get big legs like my mother!"

"Sharise," he said, his own voice low and calm, "there are people in the store."

"Her?" Sharise turned and hit Malorie with a malevolent glare.

Princess the Chihuahua was on the floor between them, watching and trembling.

Malorie tried really hard to read the story about the broken water main.

Sharise yelled at Shawn, "You need to prioritize the people in your life, *Shawn*! You need to take stock of what matters, *Shawn*!" She kept hitting his name like it was a dirty word.

The little dog started to bark, agitated that her owner was upset.

Malorie turned toward the window again and held her ground, reading her newspaper. She felt the back of her head burning, as though Sharise's hatred was physical.

Sharise ranted, Princess barked, and more of the drama unfolded. Sharise had been living with Shawn until recently, and while their recent breakup might have been mutual, she took issue with several of the things he had done since then, such as removing items that they'd bought together and talking to certain mutual friends about certain subjects that were, as far as Sharise was concerned, private between the two of them.

Yelling as she was in the middle of the ice cream shop with a stranger standing nearby trying to read about a busted water main, Sharise didn't seem that concerned about privacy.

Malorie found herself unable to read the newspaper.

Outside on the sidewalk, Bingo was getting riled up over the Chihuahua's barks and was starting to howl.

People who'd been heading toward Treat-o-Rama for an ice cream were turning around or giving it a wide berth, avoiding the screaming woman, barking Chihuahua, and howling Basset Hound.

Malorie checked her phone and noted that two hours had passed since she'd left the Half-Moon Bed and Breakfast. She set down the newspaper and left without so much as a glance back at Shawn.

She untied Bingo from his post, and they walked homeward.

Malorie said, "If Albert asks, I did try to get ice cream. You saw me, Bingo. You're my witness."

Bingo followed his nose to some interesting smells.

There were a lot of new smells on the street that day, and it would take another half an hour for them to return to the bed-and-breakfast. More than enough time for Albert to have flipped the mattress.

As they walked, Malorie wondered why any woman would ever agree to mutually break up with Shawn. He seemed like a great catch. Some people just didn't value what they had.

Chapter 3

Malorie Meyers watched TV in her room to pass the time before dinner, which started at five o'clock.

She was the first one in the dining room at five minutes after five.

Albert's partner, Bryan, greeted her warmly. Bryan was a reserved and dignified British man who, like Albert, was also sixty-two.

"Dinner smells good," Malorie said.

Bryan asked, "Have you ever had Rinderrouladen before? It's German."

"I don't think so, but I'm sure if you made it, it will be wonderful."

Bryan hadn't finished setting up the buffet yet, so he brought her a plate with three slices of meat and fillings surrounded by vegetables. The *Rinderrouladen*, also simply called roulade, was a rolled, cooked, then sliced log comprised of a thin layer of tenderized beef wrapped around a filling of bacon, onions, mustard, and pickles.

Malorie ate her meal quickly so she could leave the dining room before all the annoying happy couples arrived. They would gaze into each other's eyes adoringly then ask what she was doing there alone at the romantic bed-and-breakfast. Just thinking about having to explain her situation one more time made Malorie cringe. It was hard to take their pitying looks and harder still to hear herself rambling on and on, desperate for conversation. The only thing that had gotten her through the previous night's meal was thinking about the big stack of mail that waited for her back home on her desk.

Malorie was considering taking the risk of unwanted small talk by sticking around for dessert when someone approached her table and said, "May we join you?"

She looked up to see both Bryan and Albert, the couple who owned the place, hovering by her table. Bingo was right behind them, making the droopy Basset Hound face that matched how Malorie felt on the inside.

"Sure, guys," she said. "There's plenty of room at my table. If you have to hop up and help people, I won't be offended."

"Everyone can serve themselves," Bryan said. "That's the beauty of a buffet." He pulled a piece of beef from his plate and dropped it into Bingo's awaiting mouth.

Albert chided his partner. "You're spoiling him," he said.

Bryan said, "That's what dogs are for. And Bingo is a good boy."

"He's not *that* good," Albert said. "Malorie here had two helpings of dinner. That means she didn't go for ice cream this afternoon like we wanted her to. Bingo didn't fulfill all his duties today."

Bryan gave Malorie a sad look. "I'm sorry to hear it. We do have some ice cream for dessert."

Albert smacked Bryan on the arm. "If she didn't go for ice cream at Treat-o-Rama, that means she didn't flirt with Shawn. What a waste. If I were young and had that little body of hers, I'd be in there asking for free samples of everything, and I do mean everything."

Bryan said, "Behave yourself, Albert." Then he dropped more food into the dog's mouth.

"Guys, I did have a very refreshing walk with Bingo, who was a perfect gentleman," Malorie said. "And he did bug me to go for ice cream. I went to the Treat-o-Rama, and I did talk to Shawn, but then this horrible woman showed up and started yelling at him, so I left."

The guys exchanged a look. "Sharise Peterson," they said in unison.

Malorie asked, "What's the deal with her?"

"She's a horrible girl," Bryan said. "Sharise Peterson used to work here. We had to fire her, and we hate firing people."

"We hate it," Albert said.

"But she had to go," Bryan said.

"We don't like her," Albert said.

"I don't like her, either," Malorie said. "But it's none of my business, since I'm leaving tomorrow."

They both made sad faces.

"Promise you'll come back," Bryan said.

"Come back with a big handsome man next time," Albert said. "Someone I can flirt with to make Bryan jealous."

Bryan rolled his eyes.

Albert opened the bottle of wine he'd brought over and filled all their glasses to the brim.

Malorie said, "That's too much."

"Drink it slowly," Albert said. "And stick around a while. Don't run up to your room just yet. The night is young."

Malorie carefully took a sip. Sitting with Albert and Bryan wasn't nearly as bad as sitting by herself. She barely knew the guys, but she'd felt a connection to them immediately. They were exactly the sort of people who were suited to running a place like Half-Moon.

They drank wine, ate, and talked about the guys' adventures getting the place running.

The dining room filled up around them. Everyone raved over the roulade, and nobody asked Malorie why she was there alone because she wasn't alone.

She had Albert and Bryan and Bingo, who'd fallen asleep under the table with his chin on her foot.

Malorie checked the time. It was 6:30. She wondered where Shawn would be headed after he closed the ice cream shop. It was too bad she would never know. A more adventurous person would have taken him up on his invitation, but not Malorie. She was going to get a solid night's sleep before heading home.

The owners were whispering to each other about something and giggling.

Malorie shook her head at them. "Now what? Are you going to make me wash dishes so you can do something important in my room, like reflip the mattress?"

"We were just talking about our favorite person," Albert said. "And how, in the right light, you look exactly like her."

"And who is that?"

"Lana Langtree," Albert said.

"The country singer with the big... voice?" Lana Langtree was known for her big voice and full figure. She was getting older now, but she still did large stage shows, and she had more energy and hit songs each year than singers half her age.

"You do resemble her," Bryan said. "Have you ever considered going blond?"

"Maybe for Halloween," Malorie said with a laugh. "But even if I did, I wouldn't look like Lana Langtree." She tipped back the remainder of her wine and pushed back her chair. "Thanks for the wonderful company tonight and the compliments that I don't deserve. You two really are the best."

Albert said, "Where do you think you're going? It's not even seven o'clock, young lady."

Malorie yawned. "It's almost my bedtime."

The two looked at each other, smiled, then Albert said, "You can't go to bed until you've seen what's in the attic."

"My room is in the attic," she said.

"There's another floor," Bryan said excitedly. "You're going to love it."

She protested, but they wouldn't let her retire for the evening.

After making a round to ensure their guests had everything they needed for dinner, the two men and the Basset Hound led Malorie upstairs then through a door she hadn't noticed before, up more stairs, and into a tiny attic.

The attic had been set up as a shrine to the busty country singer, Lana Langtree. It was campy, fabulous, over the top, and perfectly suited to the famous woman.

"You really do love her," Malorie said as she admired the treasures they'd collected over the years: dresses, jewelry from charity auctions, signed photographs, and even one of her wigs. "Why do you love her so much?"

The two guys looked at each other then laughed. Albert, the flamboyant one, gushed, "She's the embodiment of love. She's a modern-day goddess, like Aphrodite but real."

The British one whacked his partner playfully on the arm. "Don't be corny. Malorie here will think we're silly." Then he said to Malorie, "Would you like to try on Lana's wig and her dress? It has magical properties." He pulled a sequined dress from a hook on the wall.

She laughed and backed away. The attic was small, so she didn't have far to go before her head bumped the angled ceiling.

Albert said, "The magic starts to work right away. Once you put on the dress, you'll feel Lana Langtree's Aphrodite goddess powers kicking in."

"I'm not sure I can handle goddess powers," Malorie said. "I couldn't even figure out how to use the complimentary clothes iron in the bathroom."

"You can handle it, honey." Albert pushed the dress at her. "Have I ever steered you wrong?"

Bryan said, "Put on that dress, and you can kiss your broken heart goodbye."

They both looked at her intently. Malorie realized how serious they were. These two kind but eccentric men truly wanted her to put on Lana Langtree's wig and dress and let the singer's goddess powers permeate her.

Albert said, "We let my sister try everything on right after a really bad breakup, and she snapped out of it immediately. She's married now." He nodded, assuring her his story was genuine. "What do they say? *Keep working on love.* They have three kids, and they still make love every day."

Bryan rolled his eyes. "Not every day. Nobody makes love every day."

"That dress doesn't look like it's my size," Malorie said.

"It's a stretch knit under the sequins," Albert said. "You can just slip it on over whatever you're wearing. The magic starts to work in only a few minutes."

Malorie had changed since her outing. She was wearing a plain black scoop-neck T-shirt over black leggings.

She was having a hard time taking her eyes off the dress, which was spectacular. Malorie would never look as glamorous as Lana Langtree did, wearing the same dress in a concert photograph that was displayed on the wall, but wasn't it worth a shot?

Perhaps if Malorie did try on the dress, and she did receive some small amount of goddess powers, maybe then Lars would realize what a mess he'd made of things. She might get back home and find him a changed man. He might get on his knees and beg for forgiveness. That wouldn't be so bad.

"Fine," she said. "I'll try on the dress."

Before she could change her mind, they were pulling it over her head. Next came the wig—big and blond. Platinum blond. It had to weigh three pounds.

Albert added some jewelry as well, "to bring out the goddess sparkle" in her eyes.

Everything had a distinctive smell to it, a perfume. Malorie wondered if the guys had sprayed the dress and wig with perfume or preservative or if that was the scent of Lana Langtree herself. Her pheromones. Her goddess powers.

The couple led Malorie to a full-length mirror and turned her around for the grand reveal.

She saw Lana Langtree in the mirror. Malorie was no longer herself but the sexy goddess of country music herself.

In the dress, her waist looked smaller and her bust looked bigger. Her hips looked perfectly proportioned.

Malorie's natural hair was a dark auburn, but she looked as natural a blonde as, well, Lana Langtree!

She turned this way and that, admiring herself. Malorie would have to do a little wig shopping of her own one day. Lars would flip if he saw her blonde like this. He'd drool all over himself, begging her to take him back.

"That should do it," Bryan said. He gently lifted the wig from her head then playfully messed up

Malorie's natural hair, which looked brighter and more appealing now.

Albert unclasped the necklace and lifted it from her neck. The goddess imprint remained. Malorie admired herself in the mirror. Had her collarbones always been so lovely?

Bryan unzipped the dress, and she stepped out of it, stepping forward toward the mirror. She was still wearing a plain black top and leggings, but she looked stunning in them.

It was as though she'd just stepped out of the darkness and into the light.

The power of Lana Langtree was all over her, radiating out of her. She imagined herself running to the ice cream store to be there at closing and then Shawn taking her in his arms and kissing her.

"Thank you," she said, trying to bring her daydreams back to Lars. It was Lars she wanted to have kissing her. "I can't wait to go home and use my new powers."

Bryan excused himself to go check on the guests. He brought Bingo with him, leaving Malorie in the attic with Albert and the memorabilia.

"Thanks for doing that for us," Albert said. "Bryan is obsessed with Lana, and you made his night. You're a good sport to play along with it and pretend you felt the goddess powers. We know it's just clothes and fake hair. My sister was going to snap out of her funk anyway."

"I do feel something, though," Malorie said. "For a minute, I actually thought about meeting up with Shawn tonight. He promised to show me around town."

Albert inhaled for a very long time, like a large balloon inflating. "You have to go," he said. "We'll stop by your room so you can put on some lipstick, and then you're going. No! Wait!" He grabbed a nearby lipstick tube that was coated in rhinestones, yanked it open, and applied it to her lips. "No stopping in your room. You're not allowed back there for... several hours. We have a... squirrel problem. There are squirrels in your room, Malorie, and it's not safe for you to go in there until after we've had the exterminator come by."

Malorie protested, but in the end, she had to admit that Albert *was* the bed-and-breakfast owner, and he knew best when it came to squirrel infestations.

Wearing Lana Langtree's signature lipstick, Malorie Meyers ran down the street toward the ice cream shop, hoping she wasn't too late.

Chapter 4

When Malorie got to the ice cream shop, the door was locked and the Closed sign was already up.

With a heavy heart, she turned around and started walking back to the Half-Moon.

A breeze brought a whiff of the Lana Langtree perfume on her skin to her nose.

As the goddess powers reactivated, Malorie turned on her heel, returned to Treat-o-Rama, and tapped on the glass.

Shawn was inside, cleaning a counter. He looked up and gave her a huge, goofy smile.

He jogged up to the front, unlocked the door, and let her in.

"I was so worried you wouldn't come," he said. "I was planning to go by the Half-Moon and beg Albert and Bryan to find you for me."

"They would have loved that," she said.

"Bingo could have helped," he said. "He's got that Basset Hound nose of his. He would have sniffed you down for sure. You can't hide from Bingo."

"No. You can't."

"I've known him since he was a puppy. He was such a cute puppy."

"I bet he was."

"I was going to get a Basset Hound from his litter, but then someone told me about a new dog at the Chihuahua rescue, and I got Princess instead." He looked down and shook his head. "I have to get her back from Sharise. What a disaster."

"I'm sure you'll get your dog back," Malorie said.

"Sharise doesn't take care of her. She's only hanging on to her to get to me."

"Sounds like you need a good lawyer."

Shawn laughed. "I'll get right on that. But first, I have to close down the till." He leaned around her and turned the interior lock for the front door. "This should keep the tourists at bay until we can make our escape."

"Just in time," Malorie said. A family of six had been approaching, with the dad pointing out that while the sign was closed, there were people inside, so they might get lucky.

Shawn gave the family a friendly wave through the glass and yelled, "Come back tomorrow! I'll give you a double scoop for the price of one!"

The dad gave Shawn a thumbs-up. The kids were not impressed. Malorie completely understood how they felt. When she'd arrived and seen the Closed sign, she'd felt the same way.

Shawn went to the staff-only area behind the counter and beckoned her to join him. As she stepped off the customer tile and onto the plain gray staff-area tile, she got a thrill from doing something most people weren't allowed to do. The tourist dad with his kids had been turned away, but Malorie was there, inside Treat-o-Rama, surrounded by ice cream and Shawn.

Shawn pushed some buttons on the cash register and said, "Help yourself to some ice cream."

"I'm pretty full from dinner."

"Then help yourself to anything you see."

Help herself to anything? She had been looking at his butt in his tight-fitting blue jeans. "I'll wait," she said.

He gave her a devilish look. "Why wait?" He abandoned the cash register, grabbed a waffle cone, and loaded it up with five miniature scoops of her favorite flavors, plus the lemon flavor she hadn't tried yet. "There's always room for ice cream," he said.

"I believe I read that on the sign on your door."

He winked at her. "And it's true."

She took a tentative lick and found it was very true.

He turned back to the cash register. "Now, where was I?"

"You haven't counted the coins yet. And you haven't put the lids on the ice cream buckets."

He let out a low whistle. "You know your way around an ice cream shop."

"I worked in one when I was a teenager. A long time ago."

"Not that long ago," he said.

She set her ice cream in one of the countertop holders then helped Shawn by putting the lids on all the flavors inside the cooler.

"That's enough unpaid labor for now," he said. "You'd better relax and eat that ice cream before it melts into a gooey puddle." He patted a white cooler next to him. "You can sit on this old thing."

She hopped up and licked her ice cream as she looked around. There were a few paperback books on the cooler, including *Catcher in the Rye* and a slim one called *Jonathan Livingston Seagull*.

Shawn counted the quarters in the cash register drawer. He dropped the coins into the drawer and said, "There's no way I can count straight with you watching me. I can't even think straight."

"I can wait outside until you're done."

"Don't you dare." He closed the till. "I'll leave a note for my brother. He's opening in the morning. Today's a special day, so he'll understand."

"It must be nice to work with family."

"You'd think." He chuckled and wrote the note. As he stuck it to the register, he said, "That girl you saw in here earlier, Sharise, she's not my girlfriend."

"Are you sure about that? She sure acted like she was."

He pulled out his cell phone and showed her a text that read: *We are OVER. XOXO Sharise*

He laughed uncomfortably as he put the phone away.

Malorie said, "Something tells me this isn't the first time you two have broken up."

He tugged at his ear and looked even more uncomfortable.

"How many times, Shawn?"

He held up three fingers, then four.

"That's tough," she said. "Nobody's perfect, and it's hard to throw away something that's pretty good most of the time." She was talking about herself and Lars, not Sharise, who was clearly *the worst*.

Shawn ran his hands through his lush, coffee-brown hair. "I keep trying to break up with her permanently." He shrugged. "I should get a tattoo to remind myself I don't want to be with Sharise. I just want to be with someone normal who appreciates me. Someone..."

"Someone you have history with," she said.

He frowned. "That wasn't what I was thinking."

"Someone you're comfortable around," she said.

"Maybe." He was still frowning. "But not too comfortable."

"Comfortable is nice. Like loungewear." She was thinking about Lars again. He would hate to know he was being compared to stretchy pants, but even he would have to admit the two were comfortable together.

Shawn asked, "What about you? When did your last relationship end?"

"Our last hiccup was about a week ago."

He raised his eyebrows. "Am I going to get beat up for taking you out on the town tonight?"

"I'm single right now," she said. "All alone. All by myself."

"Not tonight," he said.

She was still sitting on the cooler, nearly finished with the ice cream. Next, she'd eat the waffle cone.

Shawn took a step toward her. He looked at the cone and her mouth. "That looks good," he said. He took another step closer.

Malorie's heart raced. He was going to kiss her.

He got closer, and closer.

There was a loud banging on the front door.

Malorie was so startled she squeezed the waffle cone. It crumbled in her hand.

They both turned to see Sharise pointing her finger at them through the glass. Was she angry? Yes. She was. She was practically foaming at the mouth.

"Guess who's back," Malorie said.

He shook his head as though dazed. "You know, for a second, I actually did forget all about her."

Sharise kept banging on the door.

Malorie slid off the cooler and said, "I'd better get going. Is there a back door I can slip out of?"

"That way," he said, pointing toward a curtained doorway that presumably led to a back room.

"Thanks for the ice cream." She dumped the crumbled cone into a trash can under the counter. "I'll see you around. Good luck with Sharise. I'm sure her bark is worse than her bite."

He grabbed her hand. "Please don't leave. I'll deal with Sharise. Wait for me in the back room. You can't go. I think you're the only one who can help me."

She pulled her hand away from his and stepped through the curtained doorway. The back door was right there, just a few feet further.

She pushed open the back door, then let it bang shut without leaving. She found a little wooden stool and took a seat where she wouldn't be seen but could still hear what was happening up front.

Shawn opened the door. In came Hurricane Sharise.

Oh, boy, was she mad.

Apparently, she'd "accidentally" left some words out of her text message to him, and they weren't broken up, not according to her. She'd meant to say that he had to apologize to her, "or else" it would be over with them. Not that it already was.

Malorie had to give credit to Shawn. He held his ground like a man who was much older than he looked. He didn't get angry and worked up, and he didn't grovel or apologize, either.

He simply said, over and over again, "I think we should take a break from each other."

Sharise had brought Princess the Chihuahua with her. The dog barked through much of this, getting more and more worked up with Sharise's insanity.

Several painful minutes into the argument, the dog came padding back to the back room. Princess came over to Malorie, sat down at her feet, and looked up at her with the sweetest face.

"I feel sorry for you," Malorie whispered to Princess. "Poor girl. You have to live with a crazy person twenty-four seven."

The dog angled her head and gave Malorie an even more precious look.

Sharise yelled out, "Princess! Get over here! Princess! You're a bad girl!"

The dog left Malorie's feet and trotted out obediently to her owner.

Shawn said, "Don't call her a bad girl."

"It's a compliment," Sharise snapped at him. "Bad girls get what they want."

"Sharise, don't be like this."

She started shrieking, "To hell with you, *Shawn*! Why don't you go kiss your out-of-town groupie some more! Why don't you go have your fun and then tomorrow come crawling back to me!"

"Good idea," he said, his voice level. "I really do think we should take a break from each other. A long break. A permanent break."

"We'll see how you feel about taking a break tomorrow, *Shawn*!"

"Don't take Princess. She's my dog. Leave her here."

"No!"

There was the sound of her angry footsteps on the tile floor, then the front door opened and slammed shut.

Shawn sighed. Then he opened the till and started counting the change he'd tried to count before.

Malorie smiled to herself. Shawn didn't know she was there. He'd believed her door slam.

Malorie nearly giggled with excitement. She felt young again, much younger than Shawn's age, and younger than when she'd worked at an ice cream parlor as a teenager. She felt like she was ten again, playing hide-and-seek with her cousins. She'd always get so nervous, hiding in a closet behind all the coats, her heart pounding in her throat whenever anyone came near, looking for her.

She felt that same hide-and-seek excitement as she waited in the back room for Shawn to discover she was there.

Then the lights went out.

He was leaving, locking up!

Malorie jumped up and tripped over something in the dark. She grabbed a counter edge to steady herself and sent a bunch of ice cream scoops clattering across the counter than banging noisily on the floor.

Shawn called back, "Hello?"

"It's just me," she called out. "Malorie."

In the darkness, she heard him laugh in relief. "I'm so glad you're not an assassin sent by Sharise to murder me. And also, there's another thing I'm glad to hear."

The lights came back on, and he came back through the curtain to find her picking up ice cream scoops.

Grinning, he said, "I'm also relieved you said your name. I'm such an idiot. I didn't ask the first time I met you, and then it got harder to ask every time I saw you."

She extended her hand. "Malorie Meyers."

He shook it. "Shawn Gunderson," he said. "It's Swedish, but my family has been here for four generations." He gazed into her eyes. "Malorie is a pretty name for a pretty girl." He looked down at her hand, which was still in his. "You're shaking," he said.

She pulled her hand away, self-conscious. "I was scared for a minute. I thought you were going to lock me in here. Then when your brother showed up in the morning, he'd find me moaning on the floor and all the ice cream tubs empty."

He chuckled. "You would have been okay. I'm just sorry you had to hear," he nodded toward the front, "all of that nightmare drama."

She shrugged. "All of us get a little crazy sometimes. Relationships can make you question your sanity."

He raised his eyebrows and stared deep into her eyes. "Malorie, you are the most grounded person I've ever met. You came in here that first day last week, and you woke me up."

"You were sleeping?" She looked around the kitchen, which had prep space, sinks, and filing cabinets but nowhere soft to sleep.

"You woke me up in a manner of speaking," he said, taking her by the hands. "And just in time. It's my birthday today."

Malorie, who was in her thirties and feeling the age gap between them, pulled her hands away.

She didn't want to know how big the gap was, but she felt obligated to ask, "How old are you?"

"Twenty-one. As of today."

"You're just a baby," she said. "You don't want to hang out with an old lady like me on your twenty-first birthday. Where are your friends? You should be on a tour of every bar and strip club in town."

"We don't have strip clubs here."

"You know what I mean." She edged toward the back door. "I should get back to the Half-Moon. I've got to fly out early tomorrow."

"How early?"

"Seven o'clock," she said, then added, softly, "Seven p.m."

"Not exactly early," he said. "I promise not to keep you up too late tonight, but you have to join me for at least one drink. It is my birthday."

"Your *twenty-first* birthday," she said. "Shawn, I'm thirty—"

He quieted her with a finger over her lips. "All that matters is that you're old enough to not get kicked out of the bars for being underage."

"Okay," she said. "I've got that covered."

"I should warn you. We only have three bars, and one of them is karaoke."

"Sounds like fun," she said.

"Let's go." He stopped to flick off the lights then took her out the front door and locked up behind them.

The sun wasn't as hot as it had been, but the weather was still pleasantly warm.

"Phew," he said. "I'm glad I got you out of there before you melted all the ice cream."

She swatted him on the chest playfully. He stepped in, leaned down, and kissed her. Right there on the sidewalk, for anyone in town to see.

Shyly, she pulled away from him and glanced around nervously, worried about Sharise coming after them with a tire iron.

He said, "The bars won't get interesting for at least another hour, so I suggest we go to the beach and watch the sun set."

She was still swooning from the kiss.

He could have been saying anything, and she would have agreed.

For the first time during her stay in the small town, she completely forgot about Lars.

Chapter 5

Malorie and Shawn walked along the beach. He reached for her hand as they crossed some rocky terrain, and he didn't let go.

Malorie felt self-conscious about holding hands. She kept one eye open for Sharise, but there weren't many people around and no sign of Shawn's crazy ex. Gradually, she relaxed.

When he released her hand so they could cross a small river feeding into the ocean, she reached for his on the other side.

They talked about music and movies and internet culture. They weren't familiar with the same things. Malorie became even more aware of their age gap, which she jokingly referred to as a "generation gap."

Shawn laughed and said, "A decade is not a generation."

"It's a bit more than a decade," she said. "Our age difference. You don't know half the stuff I grew up with."

"There's a gap, but not a generation. We're both young people. We're basically the same age, just starting out in our adult lives."

"Says the guy who probably still lives with his parents."

"That's not fair," he said. "I'm only there temporarily. Princess and I had to go somewhere when Sharise kicked us out."

"It's good you had somewhere to go."

"Did you know my mom was out with Princess when Sharise dognapped her?"

"How would I know that?"

"You've been staying with Albert and Bryan. They know everything that goes on in this town. I'm surprised they didn't mention her."

"They may have mentioned Sharise but not anything about a dognapping."

"My poor mother was buying yarn, and when she came outside, the leash had been cut. Sharise could have untied it, but she used a knife or something, and she cut the actual leash."

"That girl has issues," Malorie said.

Shawn sighed. "She was fun when we were sixteen."

"Everyone's fun when they're sixteen. Even me."

"You're lots of fun now, Malorie Meyers."

"You wouldn't say that if you knew how excited I am to get home and open all the mail on my desk at the office."

"Well, you just told me, so now I do know, and I still think you're fun. Do you have a shiny metal letter opener?"

"I do!"

"See? You're fun."

He squeezed her hand as he helped her step over some driftwood.

Malorie couldn't stop smiling. Walking on the beach and holding hands with a twenty-one-year-old made her feel young and carefree. She felt like a teenager again, working at an ice cream shop and living each day to its fullest without worrying about tomorrow.

"Here's the best spot in town," Shawn said. He led her over to a large log, and they took a seat to watch the sunset.

After a moment, he said, "Tell me about this hiccup you had last week. Was this with the guy who was supposed to come here with you?"

"Yes. He booked the room. I thought if I came down here, he might show up, too." She looked down at the beach. She kicked off her shoes and ran her toes through the silky sand. "I'm either a hopeless romantic or a complete idiot," she said.

"You're not an idiot, so it must be the first one. Now, me, I'm an idiot because I keep getting back together with Sharise the Dognapper."

"Not anymore," Malorie said. "You're going to promise me right now that you're through. It's either that or you get the tattoo."

Shawn took her hand and placed in on his chest, over his heart. "I'll get the tattoo right here. It will be one word, Sharise, but with a circle and a line through it. Like a no-smoking sign."

Malorie liked the feeling of his warm chest under her hand, so she didn't rush to pull away. "Make sure you go to a reputable tattoo parlor, where they have good hygiene."

"What's the fun in that?" His light-blue eyes looked pale and gray in the orange sunset light. "If I get a tattoo, I want it to be done with the edge of a rusty old can."

"Tough guy, huh?"

He gazed into her eyes. "I can be tough when I need to be. Do you like what you've sampled so far?" He flexed his pectoral muscle, which was under her palm.

"You're strong," she said. "I'm impressed. That's what you want girls to say, right? 'Ooh, Shawn Gunderson, you're so big and strong!' Like that?"

"Don't stop."

He flexed his muscles again, and she giggled. "Why are you so strong?"

"Ice cream buckets are heavy," he said. "Plus I hit the gym five times a week. It keeps me sane." He tilted his face away, gazing off into the distance. "Now that Sharise is out of my life permanently, I might cut back."

"Don't cancel your gym membership yet. It's hard to permanently end things with someone you love."

"Is that how you feel about your ex?"

She pulled her hand free of his chest and looked away. "My ex," she said, unable to remember his name for a brief, weird moment. "Lars," she said. "His name is Lars."

"You have a type," Shawn said. "You like Swedish guys." He took a big breath and stuck his chest out. "Can't say I blame you. We're fun guys."

"Lars is fun," she said. "Not as fun as Sharise, but who is?"

Malorie expected Shawn to laugh, but he didn't. He asked, "What happened with you two?"

"It's more like what *didn't* happen," she said. "We were supposed to get married."

"Who broke it off?"

"I don't know," she said.

"How can you not know?"

"I was... sick at the time."

Shawn put his arm around her shoulder and pulled her close to him. "Are you cold? You looked cold just now."

"I'm fine," she said. "I was just remembering, and I guess... it's not a pleasant memory."

"You don't have to talk about it if you don't want to. Are you feeling better now?"

"I wasn't sick like that," she said. "I just threw up on myself. It only happened once."

"I shouldn't pry, but this sounds like a really good story," he said. "What happened? Were you drinking?"

"Just a little champagne," she said. "I'd only had some fruit salad and a muffin before that, so I didn't throw up very much. The dry cleaners said they might be able to get the stain out of my..." She turned her head away and mumbled words too quietly for him to hear.

He asked, "Out of your *what*?"

She turned her head back, looked straight into his open, pure, innocent, youthful eyes, and said, "Wedding dress."

His facial muscles twitched as he processed the information. After a moment, he said, "Are you saying your wedding got cancelled just because you threw up on your dress? That's a real shame."

"Plus the groom didn't show up," she said.

"Oh, Malorie." He rose off the log, swung one leg over behind him, then straddled the log so he could pull her into his embrace. "Oh, Malorie." He hugged her tight and gently rocked her from side to side. For a guy who was only twenty-one, he sure knew how to be a man.

"Thanks," she said, her voice muffled by his shoulder on her mouth. "I'm okay. Really."

"No. You're not. Is this your honeymoon? Are you here by yourself on your honeymoon?"

"No," she said then, "Yes. This was supposed to be our honeymoon."

"Oh, Malorie." He put his hands on her shoulders, pulled away, and looked into her eyes. "This Lars guy is a real loser."

"That's what some people said." Albert and Bryan had told her as much, repeatedly, and with stronger words than *loser*.

"Silly Lars," Shawn said. "Oh, well. His loss is my gain."

She tried to look away from his eyes but found she couldn't. His whole face was glowing in the golden sunset.

"Today is a special day for us," he said. "It's my birthday and your honeymoon. It's a magical day.

Fate brought us together for a reason. You're leaving tomorrow, so we only have tonight. We have to make it memorable."

"It's already been memorable, Shawn. You've been such a sweetheart to me, and—"

She couldn't finish her sentence because he was kissing her.

The sun was setting behind them.

They were the only two people on that quiet section of beach.

The waves were softly crashing behind them.

Shawn kept kissing her.

The sun set, and the night became even more magical, more memorable.

Chapter 6

Shawn and Malorie stood in front of the town's pub, an authentic-looking homage to British pubs called the Smoking Hound. Their logo was a Basset Hound in a Sherlock Holmes hat with an old-fashioned pipe.

Malorie surreptitiously pulled her shirt away from her back and removed some sand. She had sand everywhere. She didn't mind.

The pub had a sandwich board out front proclaiming tonight to be Karaoke for Lovers Night.

"They make the best burgers in town here," Shawn said, nodding toward the door. "Plus there's karaoke."

"I'm game if you are. Will you sing a song just for me?"

"I'll serenade you if you want. Though I don't know if you'll be able to respect me anymore after you hear my singing."

"I'll be the judge of that," she said, and she led the way inside.

They took a seat in a quiet corner and perused the menus. Malorie had enjoyed a great dinner at the Half-Moon, but time spent at the beach had worked up an appetite. She had a look at the appetizers and share plates.

She asked Shawn, "How do you know the burgers here are the best in town if you only just turned twenty-one?"

"It's an all-ages restaurant until later in the evening."

"So, there are only three bars in town, and you've already been to one?"

"I've been to all three," he said. "My older brother looks a lot like me, and so does his ID."

"You're bad," she said.

"Not as bad as you." He leaned in and said quietly, "I've got sand *everywhere*."

"Don't blame me. It was your idea to go skinny-dipping."

He raised his eyebrow. "Is that what we're calling it?"

The waitress arrived to take their order.

Shawn didn't take his eyes off Malorie, even though the young woman serving them was quite attractive. The waitress stared at Malorie with big eyes then scuttled off quickly.

Malorie said, "I'm guessing everyone in this town knows everyone else, right?"

"It is that sort of town."

"Then our waitress is probably sending out some text messages that are going to get back to your ex," Malorie said. "Right this very minute. Any second now, Sharise is going to know you're here with me."

"It's inevitable."

"Let's hope we get our chicken strips and beer before your ex shows up here and the fur and feathers start to fly."

"Her bark really is worse than her bite," Shawn said. "She's not *that* bad."

"Compared to what? A mythical creature?"

He scratched his head. "I don't know. She usually cools down after a good blow-up. That's how it went the other times we broke up."

"Those other times you broke up, did you ever take another girl out on the town?"

His expression clouded over. "I've only been with Sharise," he said. "Until now." He nudged her knee with his under the table.

"I'm honored to be your rebound," Malorie said. "You're a sweetheart and a gentleman. You didn't even ogle me when I was getting dressed at the beach."

"I may have snuck a peek or two. But it was under the moonlight, so it doesn't count."

"Right," she said. "Anything under the moonlight doesn't count."

He smiled and rubbed her knee with his again.

Malorie cleared her throat and looked around the pub, which was filling up with people. "It's a good thing we're seated at this table," she said. "We can keep an eye on the door. If I see your ex, I'm out of here. Is there a fire exit?" She looked around. "Is that the fire exit, or does it lead to the kitchen?"

"Just relax. Sharise isn't going to spoil our evening."

"How can you say that?"

"Nothing bad can happen to us tonight. It's our special night. My birthday and your honeymoon. It's our honey-day."

The waitress came back with their beer. This time she really took her time staring at Malorie, like she was sizing her up for a lengthy description.

After the waitress left, Shawn said, "I felt it that time. Yikes."

"She should have just taken a picture," Malorie said.

"Don't worry about her. She might know Sharise, but they're not friends. Sharise doesn't have a lot of friends."

"Aww," Malorie said, genuinely feeling sympathy for the girl. "She's probably lonely without you in her life. That would explain some of her behavior. Poor thing."

Shawn waved a finger in warning. "Don't you dare take her side. If you can't keep me on the No-Sharise path, I'll have to get that tattoo after all."

"With a rusty tin can."

"Just for the No-Sharise tattoo," he said. "When I get my Malorie tattoo, I'll visit a reputable parlor with good sanitation."

Malorie grinned and raised her beer glass to his. "Happy honey-day," she said. "Here's to reputable tattoo parlors and good sanitation."

"Happy honey-day right back." He took a drink then made a face. "Ew. Is this what beer tastes like?"

"I'm sure that's not your first beer, Mr. Twenty-One."

He winked at her then finished off half the glass.

Their food came, and they talked some more about their lives.

Shawn told her about playing baseball in high school and how a fall off his dirt bike had broken his arm, knocking him out for a season and hurting his chances at a pro career.

She asked, "If not baseball, then what are you going to do?"

"You mean when I grow up?"

She laughed into her glass of beer. "Sorry. I forgot. You're so young. You have plenty of time to figure out your life. I'm sure you won't be working at an ice cream shop forever."

"I don't need to work there now. I could hire staff to work for me full-time, but I enjoy the interaction with the customers, especially this time of year."

"You own that place?"

"Yeah," he said, giving her a sly grin. "I've got a few investments around town. Rental properties, commercial and residential, and a couple of businesses. I also own the automotive repair shop, along with my brother, who manages it."

"I had no idea."

He shrugged. "We're not billionaires or anything, but the cost of living here is low, and I want to enjoy life. Not that there's anything wrong with working hard, but I like to play hard, too."

The music that had been playing on the speakers stopped. Someone announced that Karaoke for Lovers was starting up.

Two people came on stage and started singing a duet. They were a man and a woman in their forties. They were not half bad, for karaoke.

"Karaoke for Lovers is all duets," Shawn explained. "You don't have to be lovers, and you don't even have to be a man and a woman, as long as there are two of you."

Next after the first couple was a couple of young guys—friends, not lovers, it seemed—who sang a corny duet together, much to the amusement of their friends who were seated at the front of the stage.

The waitress came by to clear Malorie and Shawn's plates. She said, "You two are up next. If you want another round, I'll have the barman hold off on pouring until after you're done singing."

"No, no." Malorie waved her hands emphatically. "We didn't sign up for a song."

The waitress pointed to another table, where the owners of the Half-Moon Bed and Breakfast, Albert and Bryan, were sitting. They both waved.

The waitress said, "Those guys picked out a song for you two. They said they'll be heartbroken if you don't sing it for them. It's one of their favorites."

"Let me guess," Malorie said. "Lana Langtree?"

"That's right," the waitress said.

Shawn said, "Of course we'll sing." He jumped up and grabbed Malorie's hand.

"I don't know if I can do Lana's songs justice," Malorie said. "I wouldn't want to ruin it for Albert and Bryan. They've been so nice to me, and they're such big fans."

"It's just one song," Shawn said. "And you only know three people in the whole town, so don't tell me you're too embarrassed. Besides, I'll be right there with you."

Malorie reluctantly followed him to the edge of the stage, where the host was standing.

The two girls who were singing a Heart song finished to a smattering of applause.

Albert and Bryan whistled and cheered from their seats.

The host told them what song the bed-and-breakfast owners had requested.

It was "Complicated Girl," a song made popular back in the 80s by Lana Langtree and a male country-and-western singer.

Shawn asked, "Do you know this one?"

She pretended to be horrified and said, "I'm not *that* old!"

"But you know it, right?"

She winked at him. Of course she did. It was a great song that was still getting played on the radio and remade by other contemporary singers.

Once they were on stage, the lights shone in their faces. Malorie was unable to see the audience, but she could hear Albert and Bryan continuing to cheer her on.

Malorie took the microphone and focused on the words on the screen in front of them and on Shawn, who was confident and relaxed.

Malorie's voice shook at first. Within a few lines, the goddess powers of Lana Langtree returned and wrapped around her, like a mystical spell. Malorie's singing improved, along with her confidence.

She knew the words by heart, as did Shawn.

By the end of the song, they were gazing into each other's eyes—really hamming it up, much to the delight of the audience.

When they finished, Shawn pulled her in for a big on-stage kiss.

Albert and Bryan hooted and hollered for an encore from the audience.

Malorie was having one of the most electrifying, exciting moments of her life. Her honeymoon had really turned around. Things were looking up.

And then someone threw a chair at the stage.

It landed inches away from Malorie's feet.

Shawn pulled her to him, and they moved to the edge of the stage just as the technician killed the spotlights.

Once the bright spots on Malorie's eyes faded, she was able to see who'd thrown the chair.

To no one's surprise, it was Sharise.

Sharise wasn't just worked up. Her face was contorted with rage. She looked like a demon, like the scariest person Malorie had ever seen outside of a horror movie.

The pub chairs had to be heavy, and Sharise was struggling to pick up another one.

A bouncer grabbed her by the arm, but he wasn't that big a guy. After one well-placed punch in the face from Sharise, he was down on the ground, clutching his bleeding nose.

Shawn yelled, "Calm down, Sharise! I would never hit a woman, but if you come at us, if you come at Malorie, you will be sorry!"

Sharise howled in outrage. She was beyond words.

Malorie spotted Princess, cowering inside Sharise's purse.

Seeing Shawn's little rescue Chihuahua in a dangerous situation turned on something primal in Malorie.

She didn't think about what she was going to do next. She just did it.

While Shawn was trying to talk to the seething rage-demon that was his ex, Malorie snuck around behind Sharise and gently lifted Princess from the bag.

Then, with the dog in her arms, she ran for the exit.

Except she had gotten turned around with all the excitement and ran instead for the kitchen.

The busy kitchen crew barely paid any attention as Malorie, who was now a dognapper, dashed through the kitchen and out a back door.

She emerged in an alley, where the night was quiet and cool.

The door slammed behind her.

Blue and red lights lit up the alley as a police car rolled by on its way to the pub.

Now what?

Princess squirmed in Malorie's arms then licked her face.

Chapter 7

Malorie Meyers wasn't alone in the alley with Princess for long.

The owners of the Half-Moon Bed and Breakfast pulled into the alley in their classic convertible.

"Your motorcar has arrived, ma'am," said Bryan, who was driving.

"Jump in quick, honey," said Albert. "The cops are coming. And Sharise, too. We can't let any of them nab you."

"I've got Shawn's dog," Malorie said. "I can't go. I'm not a dognapper."

"It's a bit late for that," Albert said, laughing. "Now hop in before you get us all in real trouble. Bring Princess. We like her."

Malorie got into the back seat, and they pulled away, the old engine roaring.

As they drove, they talked about the shenanigans they'd just witnessed.

"I hope Shawn's okay," Malorie said.

"Shawn is a Gunderson," Bryan said. "Those lads hold their own just fine."

They whizzed by the Half-Moon, which was walking distance from the town's main street.

Malorie asked, "Why did you bring your car when you two could have walked? It's only about six blocks."

Albert hopped spryly over the front seat into the back seat and said, "Honey, it's a small town. If we didn't take the car out for six-block drives, the poor old gal would just rust away in the shed." He leaned over to pet Princess and coo over her. "Who's a good girl? Not Sharise. We don't like her. But Princess is a very good girl. We like her."

"Thanks for rescuing me," Malorie said. "I was so mixed up, I would have walked off in the wrong direction and gotten lost."

"You wouldn't have gotten too far," Albert said. "It's a nice night for a drive, so we'll take the long way back home." He patted Malorie on the hand. "If we're lucky, Shawn will be waiting on the front step when we pull up."

"You think he'll know to look for me there?"

"If he doesn't, we can take a cruise by his house. I know where his folks live."

Malorie slouched in her seat, horrified at the idea she might have to meet Shawn's parents. What if they asked what she was doing with their son's dog?

Bryan glanced back and snapped, "Seatbelts! I didn't have them custom installed to not be worn!"

Albert and Malorie put on their seatbelts and settled in for a drive under the stars. The stars were so much more visible there in the small town than they were in the city.

Twenty minutes later, after circling all of town three times, they pulled up to the Half-Moon Bed and Breakfast.

Sure enough, Shawn Gunderson was waiting on the front porch.

Everyone got out of the car. Princess ran to greet her owner, barking up a frenzy.

Albert lingered. He looked like he wanted to hang out on the porch and find out everything else that had happened, but Bryan grabbed him by the hand and hauled him inside. Albert did pop his head out briefly to say, "Shawn, you're welcome to grab any empty room if you want to stick around tonight." Then Bryan yanked his partner back inside.

Malorie looked up at Shawn in the porch light. He didn't seem to have any major injuries.

"Quite the night," she said. "I hope your twenty-first birthday was memorable."

"My only complaint is we didn't get to do an encore."

"That's your only complaint?"

"It's been a magical night," he said. "You were smart to get out of there when you did. I didn't even see you go."

"I don't know if it was smart. Something came over me. Princess was so upset, and when I saw her trembling inside Sharise's bag, something snapped in me. I swear I wasn't even thinking."

"Thinking is overrated." He leaned down and kissed her. "Your lips are cold," he said. "The shock is wearing off. Around here, the nights can get chilly fast. We need to get you somewhere warm."

"It's warm inside," she said. *In my room* was implied.

"I should decline your offer," he said. "I should be a gentleman and say that you're just rattled from all the excitement of the day. I should graciously inform you that what you're feeling now you might not feel tomorrow, when you can't take it back."

"That *would* be the gentlemanly thing to do," she said.

He gazed into her eyes. "But I'm only twenty-one," he said. "I'm just a dumb kid, and I don't know any better."

"Kids will be kids," she said.

Chapter 8

Malorie and Shawn used the honeymoon suite for its intended purpose.

They didn't leave that night or the next morning, except to take Princess for a few walks. Some cans of dog food arrived at the door, accompanied by a note that it had been donated by Bingo, from his personal reserves.

At dinnertime, Malorie and Shawn shared a meal in the dining room. They arrived right at five o'clock, mindful of the impending deadline of Malorie's flight back home.

Dinner was perfect. Bryan outdid himself with a seafood lasagna that included real lobster.

Shawn knew the owners quite well. He told Malorie, "Bryan sneaks over for ice cream after he does the grocery shopping. He thinks Albert doesn't know, but he does. Albert says that Bryan enjoys the ice cream more when it's stolen, forbidden."

"Forbidden ice cream is better," she said.

"I'd give you some to take home, but it would melt." He shrugged. "I guess you'll have to stay here forever."

She turned toward the fireplace. He'd been joking all day about her staying in town. The joke was wearing thin. She'd played along in the morning, over coffee and croissants in bed on the red sheets, but now there was a part of her that did want to leave. She had things to do back home. She had all that mail on her desk. Plus there was Lars. Her heart ached when she thought about him.

Shawn said, "At least let me drive you to the airport. Let me make a fool of myself for a few more minutes."

"No, no, it's all booked. It's taken care of."

"Cancel it."

"No, Shawn. You're only going to make it more difficult for me. I'd rather say goodbye here than at the airport."

They stared at each other, at an impasse.

He said, "I can agree to that, but on one condition. You have to take Princess with you."

"Why?" Malorie's hands went protectively to the Chihuahua, who was sitting on her lap. Princess had been snuggled up with her rescuer all through dinner.

"If I have Princess, Sharise will keep stealing her back," Shawn said. "I don't need her breaking into my parents' house. My mother is still rattled from the last time Sharise dognapped Princess."

"But she's your dog. She belongs with you."

Shawn raised an eyebrow. "Then why is she snuggled up on your lap?"

"I don't fidget as much as you do."

"You love her," Shawn said. "Look into those big brown eyes right now, and tell me you don't love her."

Malorie looked down, and Princess looked up. As dog and human made eye contact, both of them did feel something. "Darn it," the human muttered.

"I called the airline when you were in the shower," Shawn said. "They've got a dog carrier you can borrow, and she can sit on the open seat next to you. If anyone asks, tell them she's an emotional support animal."

Princess wagged her tail.

"I don't know what to say," Malorie said. "You made my honeymoon magical and memorable, and now you're giving me your dog? I don't even know if my apartment building allows them."

"If anyone asks, tell them she's a large rodent, and you're a conscientious objector to extermination."

Malorie covered the small dog's ears. "You didn't hear that," she said to Princess.

Suddenly, the driver was there to drive her to the airport, and they were outside, saying goodbye.

A day earlier, Shawn hadn't even known her name, and now he was holding her tight on the sidewalk, making a scene as he promised he would always remember her, whether he got the Malorie tattoo or not.

Malorie made a vague promise to come back and visit, mentioning the travel points on her credit card. Both of them knew she didn't mean it.

Theirs was a one-day a romance, a honeymoon-birthday combo deal, and that was it. The age difference still existed, plus the thousand miles between their homes.

They managed to say goodbye, and neither of them cried.

Albert, however, was inconsolable. Bryan had to drag the man away, promising to let him watch Lana Langtree concert videos for the rest of the day.

Malorie got into the car and held Princess to the window so she could wave goodbye.

Belatedly, as she was being driven away, Malorie thought of paperwork. If she was adopting Princess officially, shouldn't there have been some sort of paperwork? When she realized that she was being silly, she laughed. When she realized she was laughing, she started to cry.

The only thing that stopped the waterworks was Princess licking her face.

The driver politely ignored Malorie's emotional breakdown in the backseat. He turned up the radio, which was playing—you guessed it—Lana Langtree. The goddess of love herself.

And so Malorie Meyers returned home with a little Princess to love.

She wasn't married or even engaged, and she sure didn't know what the heck was going to happen when she saw Lars. But she felt more hopeful than ever about her future.

Chapter 9

Malorie Meyers had an interesting trip home, with a surprising amount of male attention. She couldn't remember men hitting on her that much when she'd been engaged to Lars, but now men were drawn to her like hornets to a barbecue.

The man who sat next to her on the airplane tried to give her a neck massage. The male flight attendant doted on her nonstop. And the cab driver who drove Malorie home from the airport offered to set her up with his most attractive and wealthiest nephew.

Why all the fuss? Was it the adorable Chihuahua she had accompanying her? No. It couldn't have been Princess. Tiny dogs—even ones that weren't yappy—were not something eligible bachelors were drawn to. Older gentlemen, sure, but not guys her age.

Malorie arrived back home to her apartment late and tired.

She opened the door to find her landlord had slipped something under the door. It was a card congratulating the newlyweds and wishing them continued happiness as a couple. The landlord had handwritten a personal note: *Glad to have one less unit of sinners!*

The landlord was a friendly, easygoing guy, and his comments about the building's couples who were living in sin versus being legally wed was an ongoing joke. He'd also included a gift card for a steak dinner, on him. Along with a notice about the annual rent increase. He was a great guy, but he was still a landlord.

If Malorie had been alone, she might have opened a bottle of wine and had a good sob over the well-meaning card. But she wasn't alone. She had

Princess, who ran around the apartment excitedly, sniffing every corner. Her little brown tail went still when she found interesting smells then whipped happily whenever Malorie spoke to her.

"Do you like your new home? It might not be much, but the neighborhood is excellent. We have a lot of parks and green places for you to run around."

Princess whipped her tail, eyeballed the kitchen, and smacked her lips.

"It's bedtime," Malorie said. "Do you get fed at this time of night normally?"

Princess sat, begged, and gave Malorie the sweetest, hungriest look any dog had ever given a human.

"I don't have any dog food in the apartment. Do you eat Cheerios?"

The Chihuahua cocked her head.

"Forget the Cheerios. We're out of milk anyway." Malorie parked her suitcase in the master bedroom and pulled on a sweatshirt. "Wait here. I think the corner store is open. They sell dog food at corner stores, don't they? Why am I asking you? I'm basically talking to myself, aren't I? Don't answer that. I'm sure the corner store will have something. Hang tight, and I'll be back in fifteen minutes."

Malorie opened the apartment door. Princess scampered out into the hallway, tail wagging.

"Oh," Malorie said. "I guess you can come with me. That's what people with dogs do, isn't it?"

She grabbed the plain black leash the airline had provided and snapped it to the dog's sparkling rhinestone collar.

Outside, the summer night air was brisk and refreshing. Not as warm as where she'd been on her honeymoon, but the weather was warming up for summer. Malorie lifted her face to the sky. It had very few visible stars but was still beautiful. She had only been inside the apartment for five minutes, but on the trip out again, it felt like a completely different night.

Maybe it *was* a completely different night.

Five minutes earlier, she'd been a tired woman coming home from a late flight.

Now she was someone else. Not a newlywed but a new dog owner, on a mission to find dog food. She was responsible for someone besides herself. She was not alone in the world.

They stretched their legs on the walk to the corner store. Princess kept up really well on her short legs.

The store was open—it rarely closed—but they didn't allow pets inside. Malorie tied Princess to the bike rack and went in. She felt strangely empty-handed without the leash in her hand.

The store was empty except for the staff and one customer.

A man in a big coat was laughing at something the clerk told him. He had a big, loud laugh that filled the place.

Malorie located the dog food and selected one can each of five types of food. Then she changed her mind, put back the large, economy-priced can, and grabbed three of the smaller, pricier tins. The label said they were gourmet. Nothing but the best for Princess!

She stopped to picked up some milk from the dairy cooler and realized something. From that day forward, Malorie would never again wake up without fresh milk in the fridge. Not if she took Princess for a before-bed walk every evening, past the convenience store on the way to the park. That was a perk. Dog ownership had a lot going for it, she thought pleasantly, and she was only on her first day.

The loud man who'd been at the counter left, and Malorie plopped the cans on the checkout counter.

"These are for my dog," she said proudly. "I just got her. I'm a dog owner."

The clerk, who, until now, had only known Malorie as the lady who rushed in for milk in the mornings, pretended to be interested. "Dogs are cool," she said. "I like dogs."

"She's a Chihuahua," Malorie said. And then, trying out a phrase she'd heard many times before, she added, "She's a rescue."

The clerk said, "Aww. A rescue Chihuahua sounds adorable. What's her name?"

"I didn't name her," Malorie said self-consciously. "She came with a name, and I didn't want to freak her out by changing it. She's right out there. That's Princess." Malorie pointed to the glass doors.

Both she and the clerk looked outside just in time to see the loud man with the big coat walking away with Princess.

The clerk said, "Uhhh."

Malorie didn't hear the rest because she was running out the door.

She ran while yelling at the man's back, "Stop, thief! That's my dog! Stop! Dog thief!"

The man stopped and turned. In a thick Russian accent he said, slowly and in a deep, booming voice, "Dog is not yours. Dog is mine."

She stopped a few feet away from the stranger and adopted a fighting stance. "You can't steal people's dogs. Give her back right now and I won't call the police on you. Just hand the leash over and we can forget all of this."

The man lifted his free hand and glanced around, as though looking for witnesses to the craziness he was witnessing. Craziness that he hadn't caused.

"You call police? No, I think you do not. Dog is mine. You want money? Okay. I give money."

"The dog is not for sale," she said. "Just give her back. I don't want your money."

"One thousand dollars," he said, reaching for his wallet.

"No way! She's not for sale. Not even for a million dollars."

He grinned. "Good. I have only forty dollars." He pulled the money from his wallet and held it out between them. "Here. Forty dollars. Enough to make you go away?"

"I want my dog."

"*Not* your dog."

"Princess," Malorie called to the dog. "Come here, girl."

Princess was smelling a lamp post and paying zero attention to what was going on.

"Dog does not know you," the man said. "Please, take money. Buy a hot meal. If you need somewhere to sleep tonight, maybe I help. I know people."

"I don't need anywhere to sleep tonight. I just want my dog back so I can go home to my apartment. It's been a long day, okay?"

"You have apartment? You are not homeless? Where is purse?"

Malorie patted her shirt, which was the paint-speckled one Lars used for painting the apartment. Where was her purse? It had to be on the counter of the convenience store, along with the cans of dog food and jug of milk.

"Never mind about my purse," she said defiantly. "It's somewhere safe. Now give me my dog back before I..."

"What?" He grinned. He had light-blue eyes, and they twinkled under the street light. He wasn't nearly as old as his voice. Maybe forty. And not unattractive. What was a handsome guy doing stealing dogs?

It didn't matter. He wasn't getting Princess. Not on Malorie's watch.

In her next breath, Malorie found herself channeling another female's energy. Not Lana Langtree the country music superstar. It was a different sort of energy. It was a Sharise Peterson energy. Shawn Gunderson's ex.

Malorie smacked her hand into her open palm, Sharise style, and said, "Before I make you sorry. You don't know me, Mister, but I am one crazy broad, and you do not want to mess with me. I can throw a heavy chair ten feet onto a stage, and I can take down a bouncer with a single well-placed punch. I've got... a particular set of skills." She smacked her hand a second time for emphasis.

At that moment, Princess suddenly recognized something. It must have been her former owner's energy. The Chihuahua came running to Malorie's feet. The leash pulled free of the man's hand and trailed behind her. Princess was not a yappy dog, but she did let out one yip of excitement.

Malorie scooped up the dog in her arms and held her protectively.

"That collar," the man said. "It has diamonds?"

"They're just rhinestones," Malorie spat at him. "Is that why you stole her? You thought she was wearing diamonds? You are one dumb criminal, you big Russian thug!"

"Dog is female?"

"What else would a dog named Princess be?"

"I did not know," he said.

She backed away slowly. "If you ever mess with me or my dog again, Boris, you will be sorry."

He held one hand to his chest. "Boris? Me? You try to hurt my feelings, but Boris is good, strong name. Do you want real name? I have business card." He reached into his wallet again.

"Sure. I'd love your card, so I can pass it along to the police."

He slowly tucked the wallet and white business card back into his pocket.

When he spoke next, the thick Russian accent and broken English were gone. He spoke clearly, with only a slight accent. "Listen, lady. I know this must look really bad to you, but it was all a misunderstanding, I swear."

"Where's your accent?" She glanced around wildly. "What kind of scam is this?"

"No scam," he said, sounding sincere. "I thought you were a homeless person. Doing my impression of my grandfather usually does a good job of scaring people like that off." He took a step toward her.

Malorie took two steps back. If she'd had pepper spray in her pocket, the Russian, whatever his name was, would have gotten a face full of it.

"I'm sorry," he said. "I made a mistake."

"You sure did," she said.

Then she whirled around and ran back to the safety of the convenience store as quickly as she could.

The clerk had her purse, her tins of dog food, and the milk, all packed and ready to go. It was a good neighborhood, where things like dognappings didn't usually happen.

Malorie relayed the story of what had happened. The clerk was horrified. She claimed to know nothing about the Russian, except that he'd been coming in every night or two for the past week.

Malorie returned to her apartment, fed Princess, and set up a bed for her.

She didn't think she'd be able to sleep at all, but she did.

In the morning, Princess was the very definition of bright-eyed and bushy-tailed, ready to greet the day.

Malorie got dressed for work then enjoyed her Cheerios with milk while Princess dined on her gourmet dog food.

"You can't stay here in the apartment all day," Malorie said. "What if the Russian comes looking for you? Lars must have taken his fancy security system with him when he moved out."

Princess cocked her head and let out a single yip.

"That could be a problem," Malorie said. "I can't have you barking like mad in here and getting us evicted. The landlord barely tolerates people living in sin. He's not going to be happy about me having a dog in here. You'll have to come with me to work."

Princess said nothing.

"Work is fun," Malorie said. "It gives you something to do so the days don't get too long. There are other people around to talk to and free coffee. Plus they pay you."

She opened the door, and Princess ran out ahead.

The landlord was in the hallway, changing a light bulb. Princess scampered directly to him and jumped up, pressing her front paws into his calf as she gave him a friendly bark of greeting.

Chapter 10

Lars Lundin

While Malorie Meyers was trying to convince her landlord that a Chihuahua was barely even a dog and therefore allowable under the building rules, across the city, Lars Lundin was trying to figure out how to use a very complicated shower.

There was a tap on the bathroom door. A woman called in sweetly, "Did you figure it out? You have to push the button in while you rotate the handle."

"I know how a shower works," he replied tersely.

"Don't break it," she said. "It breaks easily."

"Don't hound me, woman! If you don't like how I'm doing it, come in here and do it yourself!"

The door opened. Yuki Noguchi, the owner of the shower, came in, looking small and adorable in a silky robe.

"Silly boy," Yuki said, leaning past him to turn on the shower then adjust the temperature. "You're a genius when it comes to electronics and wiring, but you can't figure out a shower."

"Not a foreign shower, with everything hooked up backwards." His tone had softened, but he was still grumpy. Lars was not a morning person, and he didn't respond well to criticism, which was how he viewed all offers of help.

Yuki wrapped her arms around his back and snuggled her face to his chest. She was a foot shorter than him, and her nose was basically in his armpit. His armpits were as stinky as his morning mood, but Yuki didn't mind. They were in the early honeymoon phase of a new romance, and her bonding hormones were running high enough to allow her to ignore all of Lars's flaws, such as the fact he had left his fiancée at the altar a little more than a week earlier.

Lars kissed Yuki on the top of her head. Her hair was black and silky, like the robe. Everything about Yuki was silky. She was such a change from Malorie, who was like natural organic cotton with a spandex blend.

Yuki held him tighter, and her robe slipped to the floor.

Lars might have thought about Malorie and the fact she was back in town and the fact he had to come clean with her, but Yuki was *so* silky. His brain could only focus on one thing at a time.

"Thanks for letting me stay here," he said. "Your apartment is nice, except for the stupid shower."

"I'm glad you like it here. You don't ever have to leave, my big, strong Viking."

He flexed his upper-body muscles to display his Viking strength.

Yuki climbed into the shower with Lars. She gave him a tutorial on the temperature and pressure settings, among other things.

Chapter 11

Malorie Meyers

Malorie strolled into work with her new Chihuahua. Princess showed no fear or trepidation about the new environment. She did pause to bark at the big dog in Paul's office. Paul was the accountant, and he brought his pooch to work regularly.

Paul's dog, a brown Labradoodle named Pedro, bounded out to greet Princess. They sniffed each other while running in circles. Paul came to the doorway and leaned against it.

"Malorie, I'm so sorry about the you-know-what," Paul said. "Everyone's really sorry." Paul was thirty-one, single, and matched his Labradoodle in hair and temperament. Paul and the rest of the staff at the small company had been invited to the you-know-what, the wedding that didn't happen.

"I hope you all stayed and ate the food," Malorie said. She hadn't stuck around herself, but the hired wedding coordinator had passed along the message that people shouldn't go home if they didn't want to.

"The Lundin clan left with their tails between their legs," Paul said. "As they should have."

"They didn't do anything wrong."

"They didn't do everything right raising Lars, now, did they?"

Malorie looked away from Paul's empathetic expression. "I don't want to talk about it," she said. "How was the dinner?"

"Most of us stayed, since we knew you would have wanted us to. Penny got wasted. She was dancing on tables."

Penny was their boss, the owner of the company. Malorie couldn't picture Penny dancing, much less on a table.

"Life is strange," Malorie said. "Just when you think you have it figured out, it gets stranger."

They both looked down at the dogs. "I'll say," Paul said. "Who is this, anyway? Are you looking after her for a friend?"

"She's mine. Long story. A guy gave her to me so his ex wouldn't keep dognapping her." Malorie frowned. "I guess that wasn't such a long story."

Paul clapped his hands in delight. "That's one of my favorite things! When long stories aren't long. It's almost as good as when people sing with the radio on road trips."

"In real life or in comedies?"

Paul ruffled his brown curls and gave her a serious look. "Life *is* a comedy, Malorie," he said. "You have to see it that way, or you'll be depressed all the time."

"Do you say that because you're an accountant?"

"I love accounting," he said, his eyes wide with surprise. "I love everything about it, especially how every number adds up to what it's supposed to be."

"I love my work, too," Malorie said.

"It's the rest of life that's challenging," Paul said. "Work is easy."

"Work is fun," Malorie said. "It keeps you busy, there are people around to talk to, and free coffee."

"I'm glad you understand," Paul said. "All my other friends do is complain about their careers. Sometimes I wonder if they're the problem, not the job. Look at the two of us with our jobs that we love. We work at the head office for a company that manufactures sportswear for people to wear on the couch. It's not like we're saving lives or anything."

"We're very lucky," Malorie said. "Plus our boss gets wasted and dances on tables, apparently."

"It keeps getting better," Paul agreed. The fact that employees could bring their dogs to work went unmentioned.

Paul walked back around his desk, got a dog treat, and broke off a small piece for Princess. After a few more minutes of fawning over the Chihuahua, he allowed Malorie to leave for her desk. Before she could reach her chair, Paul ran up, puffing and holding a dog bed. A very large dog bed. "Pedro sleeps on my couch like a spoiled brat anyway, so Princess can have his bed."

"We'll just borrow it until I can get a smaller one," Malorie said. "Thanks, Paul. You're the best."

Paul started shoving the large dog bed into place under Malorie's desk. It barely fit. Princess knew exactly what it was for without being told. She made herself right at home.

A minute later, Malorie was in The Zone, that peaceful state she got into whenever she had a satisfying amount of straightforward work to get through.

The stack of unopened letters and packets that had been waiting on her desk—the stack she'd fantasized about to hold back tears on her honeymoon—was even taller that she'd imagined. Brandishing her shiny silver letter opener, she immersed herself in the task, ripping through envelopes and sorting everything into piles for the next step.

Life had its ups and downs, but the mail kept coming. It was good to be able to count on something.

Malorie was a fashion designer, technically, but it wasn't exactly a life of endless glamour. She was also the assistant to the owner, Penny. Malorie did a lot of entry-level work, including answering emails and setting up phone calls. Penny and Malorie were close enough that Malorie knew Penny and her husband were trying for a baby. Penny had hinted that Malorie might take over more duties if and when Penny went on maternity leave. After that, the promotion could become permanent. The company did like to promote from within.

The name of the company was Penntastic, as was their line of sensible, comfortable clothes that came in a wide range of colors and sizes. The plus-size range had been performing well, but the tall line was also holding its own. Tall women loved the extra-long, extra-stretchy leggings the company was known for.

Some of the people at Penntastic were workaholics, and others were what Malorie would lovingly call "eccentric," but they were all fun people. The owner, Penny, came from old money and had married into new money. The clothing label had started as Penny's vanity project, a hobby alternative to charity lunches with the other wealthy ladies. Nobody was more surprised than Penny's husband when the label took off and started making money instead of costing money—not that she and her husband needed it.

Penntastic operated out of a renovated warehouse in the brewery district, with the offices and design facilities sharing the same building. Actual production was done overseas, though they were always on the verge of setting up a factory locally.

It was nearly lunch, and Malorie was sorting fabric samples for Penny, looking for a specific shade of teal, when her cell phone beeped with a message.

It was Shawn, checking to see that Princess was settling in.

Malorie: *She's hanging out under my desk in a bed that's big enough for a dozen Princesses.*

Shawn: *I miss her already.*

Malorie sensed he meant more than he was saying.

Malorie: *She misses you, too. You were good to her. You rescued her when she needed it.*

Shawn: *She's going to be just fine. Her future is wide open. She's one tough cookie. I was there, in the right place at the right time, but she barely needed me.*

Malorie: *She appreciates you, all the same.*

Shawn sent her the emoji for a thumbs-up, and that was the end of it.

Lunchtime came, and Malorie took Princess outside for a walk in the small park next to the building. Paul was there with Pedro and provided plastic bags for that trip, plus a few more to keep Malorie in supplies until she could visit the pet store.

"I don't need that many," Malorie said, trying to give some back.

"Trust me. You do. Dogs defy the laws of physics. It doesn't matter how much they eat. There's always another present coming your way that needs gift wrapping."

"You have a wonderful way of phrasing things, Paul."

He gave her another one of his serious looks. "What about us, Malorie? Me and you? Do you think there's a chance, now that you-know-who is out of the picture?"

She laughed and jokingly pushed him away. He didn't budge. Paul was more solid than he looked. He stood there in his sweater vest, looking at her with his puppy-dog face.

"You're too young for me," she said.

"I'm almost thirty-two."

"But you're..." She couldn't put it into words. "You're so... *Paul*."

He sighed and rolled his eyes. "I know. There's not much I can do about that." He shrugged. "I had to ask." He glanced around to make sure nobody was within earshot then said, "At your you-know-what, Penny made me promise I would ask you out. People are worried about you. Everyone feels really bad about what happened."

"Our boss made you promise to hit on me? Now, there's an interesting sexual harassment case."

Paul stumbled backward awkwardly, arms waving. "No, no, no," he said. "I didn't mean—"

"Relax," she said. "I think it's sweet that everyone was concerned about me."

"If they ask, tell them I was very subtle about it."

"I hope they don't ask," she said. "I don't want to talk about it ever again. Even in the future, if Lars wants to tell the story for our grandkids, I'll beg him not to. I know tragedy plus time equals comedy, but it's my life, too."

Paul grimaced and sucked in air between his teeth. "Yikes," he said.

"I'm fine," Malorie reassured him. "It was just a hiccup."

Paul frowned. "Do you actually think that you and Lars are going to get back together after what he did?"

"He got cold feet," Malorie said. "It happens. We've broken up a bunch of times, and we always come back stronger than ever." She looked down at Princess, who was kicking up grass next to her second gift delivery that day. "Of course, he never moved all of his stuff out of the apartment before."

Paul placed a hand on Malorie's shoulder. "I think it's over. I don't mean to be cruel, but when you add up all the columns, the numbers add up one way. What's that saying? *He's just not that into you*." He grimaced. "Did I actually say that out loud? I'm so sorry."

"I appreciate your concern," she said. "How about you worry about your love life and I'll keep tabs on my own? Hey, speaking of which, how are things going with Yuki?"

Yuki Noguchi worked in the pattern-making department, and Paul had been lovesick over her since the day she'd started at the company a year ago. Yuki was beloved by all who knew her. Yuki wasn't any more friendly or outgoing than the rest of the Penntastic crew, but she was one of the most complimentary people Malorie had ever met. She had a way of making everyone feel wonderful and smart and capable. Part of it was the nicknames she gave everyone.

Within a day of having met Paul, she'd started calling the solid, somewhat bland accountant Pedro's Big Daddy. Paul ate it up with a spoon.

Paul gazed off into the distance. "We danced together at your wedding. I mean, at the you-know-what."

"Good for you!" She clapped him on the back. "That's something, isn't it?"

Paul looked down, frowning. "It was one of those songs where everyone was dancing," he admitted.

"Hang in there," Malorie said. "She'll come around eventually. One day, she'll see you as more than Pedro's Big Daddy."

Paul beamed upon hearing the flattering nickname.

Malorie was glad to see Paul smiling, but she did feel a tiny bit bad for lying.

There was *no way* Yuki was ever going to take an interest in Paul. He was decent, but he wasn't exactly the pick of the litter. Yuki was the sort of independent, single woman who was only single by choice. Women like Yuki Noguchi could have any man their hearts desired and knew it. Heaven help the girl who stood in the way of a woman like that!

Chapter 12

Tuesday

Malorie Meyers stepped up to the counter at the dry cleaner's and handed over her ticket.

"You're the bride," said the short, dark-haired woman working there. "The bride who threw up all over her dress."

"That's me," Malorie said. Being called *the bride who thew up on her dress* was not flattering, but it was better than being called *the bride who got left at the altar.*

"Congratulations," the woman said. "How was the honeymoon?"

"Surprising," Malorie said.

"Good for your husband!" The woman went to retrieve the dress. When she came back, she proudly said, "The stain is all gone. It is as good as new. You can pass it down to your daughter. See you again in twenty years!"

"You may see me sooner than that," Malorie said. When she and Lars finally did tie the knot, she'd get the dress cleaned again for storage.

"We have a special on blouses next week." The woman handed her a coupon and wished her a nice day.

Malorie went home and hung the dress in her closet. Not at the back but in the middle, where it was accessible. Just in case.

Chapter 13

Malorie's first week back at work went well enough, considering people kept stopping by her desk to make sympathetic expressions and pry for more information about her life. Everyone wanted to know, why *had* her wedding to Lars Lundin been cancelled at the last minute?

Malorie kept saying, "I really don't know. Everything was all set up and ready to go, and then Lars must have gotten cold feet. That's a thing that happens sometimes."

That answer satisfied no one.

"Ask Lars yourself if you can get a hold of him," Malorie said. "He's not answering his phone, and he's not at the shop." Lars owned a company that installed custom car stereos in high-end vehicles.

Whenever Malorie called the shop, his employees reported that he wasn't around or had just stepped out. They did the same when she stopped by unannounced. When she was there in person, the staff were all wide eyes and nervous sweats. She had a strong intuition they were lying.

Lars would have a *lot* of explaining and groveling to do when they got back together.

Until then, at least she had Princess to keep her company. Then, down the road, the three of them would make an adorable family of three. Until they became a family of four, five, or maybe more.

Malorie had taken Princess to a vet on Thursday and had been reassured that the dog was still young. Princess had plenty of fun-filled, healthy years ahead to play with the plump-cheeked Lundin babies whenever they came along.

On Friday afternoon, Malorie finished writing all her notes to herself for Monday—she liked to think of Monday Malorie as a completely different person —and packed up to go home.

When she walked outside, the object of Paul the Accountant's crush, Yuki Noguchi, was standing outside the front door of the building. She was smoking an impossibly long cigarette.

"Yuki!" Malorie exclaimed. "I haven't talked to you all week. You must be avoiding me," she joked.

Yuki dropped the long, barely-smoked cigarette and crushed it under her boot. Smiling with all her teeth visible, she looked down at Princess and said, "I don't like dogs."

"But you love Pedro."

"I don't like *little* dogs," she said. "They're small, which makes them fast and scary. Like the fast zombies instead of the slow zombies."

"Princess is harmless." Malorie picked up the Chihuahua and held the dog aloft. "Look at that adorable little face."

Princess, who was not a yappy dog, began barking furiously.

The petite, dark-haired woman backed away. "Another time," she said. "I've got to get going. But we should definitely catch up next week, so you can tell me how your trip went." She walked away backward at a brisk pace. "We'll do lunch!"

Malorie used her hand to make Princess wave goodbye. The dog had stopped barking like a lunatic and was only growling. Spit was flying out of her tiny mouth.

Malorie set the dog down and asked, "What's gotten into you? We had a week of perfect behavior, and now that it's the weekend, you're doing your impersonation of a hellhound?"

Princess stopped growling, but her lip stayed stuck, giving her a manic snaggletooted look.

"What am I going to do with you?"

The dog tilted her head.

"Do you want to stop by the stereo shop on the way home and see if Lars is ready to meet you yet? He's going to be your new doggy daddy."

The dog snorted and shook her head. It looked like a no, but Malorie wasn't sure.

Then the dog did it again.

"Fine," Malorie said. "We can pop in on Saturday. The shop's always busy then, and he'll be on the floor for sure."

Chapter 14

Later on Friday night, Malorie took Princess for the last walk of the evening, which included a visit to the Quick Stop.

There was a ruckus going on across the street at O'Flannagan's Pub, so Malorie did something she never thought she'd do. She picked up the Chihuahua and tucked Princess into the new shoulder bag she'd purchased online and had shipped to her apartment.

Princess settled in immediately. Malorie entered the Quick Stop with a dog stowed in her purse and her head held high. Stores had no right to dictate what a woman carried inside her purse. It was between that woman and her purse. It was personal!

The clerk called out, "Hi, Malorie. Hi, Princess."

Malorie immediately caved on her brave stance. She ducked her head and apologized for trying to smuggle the dog into the store.

The clerk, whose name was Justine, said, "Don't worry about it. After the crazy Russian tried to steal her, I can't blame you for not wanting to leave her tied up outside."

Malorie and Justine had been chatting nightly since the attempted abduction. They were on a first-name basis now. Justine didn't know it, but that limited amount of connection put her in the top ten list of Malorie's best and closest friends.

Malorie grabbed more dog food, milk, and some crackers.

At the checkout, Justine said, "Speaking of the crazy Russian, he's been in here a lot lately."

"Lucky you."

"And he asked about you again."

"Ugh," Malorie said. "That's all I need. A stalker of my very own." She didn't say it, but the part of her that wasn't terrified at the prospect did feel flattered.

Justine handed her a business card. "That's from him," she said. "He gave me one, too."

The card was for a free ice cream cone and unlimited toppings.

"You've got to be pulling my leg," Malorie said. "Am I on a hidden camera show? Did the Gundersons set this up?"

Justine, who wasn't the type to question who or what the Gundersons might be, said, "I already cashed mine in today. It's right up the street from here."

"We don't have an ice cream shop around here. Trust me. I'd know about it if we did."

"You know that vacant storefront next to the place with the giant teapot?"

"Next to Delilah's? Yes, I think I know which store you mean."

Justine tapped the card. "It's a pop-up shop, only here for the summer. They set it up in about three days flat. I guess they do this sort of thing all the time. They're using Baker Street to roll out some sort of marketing research for an ice cream company."

Malorie looked at the card again, hoping the logo was for Treat-o-Rama, Shawn's ice cream shop.

The logo was actually for Butter Spoons.

"Butter Spoons," Malorie said. "Never heard of it."

"That's probably why they're doing the research," Justine said. "I think the crazy Russian guy must work there."

"Or he stole these free ice cream cards off someone who does."

Princess, who sensed she'd been forgotten about, let out a single yip from the purse.

"We'd better finish our walk," Malorie said. "I promised she could take her time at the park, since it's not a weeknight and we can sleep in tomorrow."

"Smell everything," Justine said to the dog. "Smell it twice."

Malorie paid for the food, wished Justine a great night, and stepped outside.

On the way to the park, Malorie passed under the giant teapot sign for Delilah's then stopped to peer in the window at Butter Spoons, the pop-up shop that had set up on Baker Street for market research. The interior was clean and minimal, with none of the 1950s kitsch people usually put in ice cream parlors. Probably because they'd set up shop in three short days. Even so, it didn't look bad.

Big signs on the windows boasted about the incredible selection as well as the health benefits of Butter Spoons ice cream, which was made with organic ingredients and catered to a variety of dietary needs. There was traditional farm-style ice cream, plus lactose-free ice cream, vegan ice cream, and several low-carb options sweetened with stevia or xylitol. The base flavor was vanilla, and the flavoring variety came from the various toppings. It was similar to the place with the chilled marble slab but without the slab gimmick.

Malorie and Princess continued on their walk.

At the park, Malorie tossed the card for the free ice cream into the trash can.

She didn't want anything from the crazy Russian.

She did want ice cream, though. She would come down Saturday afternoon and treat herself to a cone or sundae, but she would pay for it herself.

If she saw any sign of the crazy Russian, she would stow Princess in her purse and run away.

Chapter 15

Saturday

On Saturday morning, Malorie had a healthy breakfast in her apartment and waited a very reasonable two and a half hours before heading out for ice cream at Butter Spoons.

Walking in and being hit with the scent of vanilla and cream reminded her of Shawn. Had it already been a week? She nearly turned around and walked back out, but the teenagers working behind the counter looked nervous or eager or a combination of both.

There were three of them lined up in a row. "Welcome to Butter Spoons," they said in unison.

"At ease," she said jokingly. "I live in the neighborhood. Folks are used to a more casual approach to customer service around here."

The boy on the end saluted her. "Yes, ma'am."

The girl in the middle began pointing at the flavors and delivering a practiced speech about the "Butter Spoons way."

After some deliberation, Malorie selected the Angelic base. It was both low-carb and vegan, made with coconut milk. She topped it with the Devilish topping, which was a combination of treats that were anything but low-carb or vegan.

"That's our most popular combination," said the rosy-cheeked boy working the cash register. "People are weird, huh?" He punched a button and named the total.

A booming voice came from the back of the shop. "No pay! No pay for the lady!"

A man emerged from behind a gingham curtain. It was the crazy Russian. Either he'd mugged an employee and stolen their apron, or he worked there.

"I'm paying," Malorie said, avoiding eye contact with the crazy man. "I don't want anything from you." She heard the acid in her voice and added, "No offense."

The Russian boomed, "If you pay, it is a great offense!" He reached over the employee and closed the cash drawer. "No pay."

Malorie looked over her shoulder and checked that Princess was still safely tied up outside the shop. It was the fifth time she'd checked since walking in.

She reached for the ice cream, a sundae, but the man grabbed it from the other side and yanked it back.

"You," he said. "I have something you must see."

She stepped back, waving both hands. "No, thank you. Nuh-uh. No way."

The man whistled. The gingham curtain shook, and a brown Chihuahua emerged from under the hem.

Malorie shoulder checked. Princess was still outside.

"This is Duke," the Russian said, no longer booming. His thick accent all but went away as he said, "This is what I meant about the other night being a misunderstanding. I left Duke in the apartment when I went out for some potato chips, and when I stepped out of the convenience store, I must have grabbed the leash for your dog out of habit."

Malorie was stunned by the revelation. When she found her words, she said, "You should have said that at the time."

"I tried," he said. "I told you it was my dog."

"But it *wasn't* your dog. You were mistaken."

"In any case, you have to admit you were part of the problem."

"Me?"

"It all would have gone much easier if you hadn't looked the way you did."

She considered how she might have appeared that night and how the whole thing seemed almost hilarious when framed in this new light. Almost, but not quite. And now he was insulting her appearance?

"Sorry, Boris. You're not pinning this on me," she said.

"Think about it from my perspective. To me, you looked like you were the mad one," he said. "No offense."

She snorted. Offense had definitely been taken. "I'd had a long day. A very long day. Nobody looks completely sane after a flight with turbulence, especially not after sitting next to a guy who keeps offering to give you a neck massage."

The Russian turned to the trio of young staffers, who were watching the conversation as though it was an informational video being played as part of their training.

"Work now," he said, utilizing the thick accent. "If you have time to lean, you have time to clean. Chop chop." He reached down and fastened a leash onto his dog's collar. He said to the trio, "I take nice lady for walk in park. When I come back, all ice cream has been sold."

The trio jumped into action and cleaned nervously.

The man still had Malorie's sundae in his hand as he led the way outside.

They stopped by Princess, and he said, in a much milder voice, "They all know the accent is fake, but it sure gets them moving."

Duke sniffed Princess. The dogs yipped at each other like old friends.

Malorie bent down and tried to pet Duke, but he wouldn't hold still.

The two dogs ran in excited circles, checking each other's smells.

Seeing them side by side, the differences between the two were obvious. Princess was smaller, and her coloring was more caramel than Duke's chocolate. But when Duke had come running out of the back room, Malorie really had checked over her shoulder. A person could mix up the dogs if they weren't expecting a look-alike.

Malorie and the Russian continued standing in front of the ice cream shop while people walked by. It was much more comfortable being around him in the daytime, with people around and without him trying to steal her dog.

She got a better look at him in the sunshine. The Russian had ice-blue eyes and dark hair, cut very short. He had a widow's peak, which gave him a heart-shaped face. His jaw was strong, and his chin jutted forward, like the man in the-moon in storybooks. He looked about forty, give or take. No wedding ring. Not that it mattered, but she'd noted the absence of any jewelry.

As they stood there, silently observing the dogs, he removed his white apron and stuffed it into a back pocket. He wore a tight-fitting sports shirt, dark blue, like the kind runners wore. He was broader than a runner, though, with solid muscles and Popeye forearms. His arms were hairy, but not *too* hairy. Not that it mattered how hairy his forearms were or were not!

The dogs settled down and looked up at their owners expectantly.

Malorie looked at her ice cream, which was still being held by the not-so-crazy Russian and was melting in the sun.

"Thanks for the free ice cream," Malorie said. "Just let it dribble all over the sidewalk. That's how I like it."

He smiled. "Sarcasm. I like it." He handed her the sundae and urged her to eat it quickly.

She took a slow, deliberate bite.

He lifted up his chin and watched with his upper lip raised, as though he might be able to taste it through empathy.

She took another bite, then waved her spoon as she talked. "It's good," she said. "And I'm good. Honestly. I don't need any more of an explanation. It's very clear that what happened the other night really was a misunderstanding. I'm sure if you'd been a little faster and gotten Princess all the way back to your place, you would have come right back and found me."

"Who can say," he said in the thick accent. "One dog is good. Two dogs is... two dogs. Twice as good, no?" He gestured for them to start walking. "Park is this way, yes? No?"

"Something tells me you already know the answer to that question, yes? No?"

He smiled at her impression of his exaggerated accent.

He took both of the dogs' leashes so she could have her hands free for eating. "Don't worry. I won't mix them up. Yours has the diamonds on the collar."

"That's right. A million dollars' worth of genuine diamonds. Nothing but the best for my girl."

As they walked, he handed her a business card. This one didn't promise a free ice cream, but it did have a name: Sacha Mikhelson, CEO, Butter Spoons.

"Sacha," she said. "So, you *are* Russian, but the accent varies as needed."

"Now you know everything there is to know about me. What is your name and your accent?"

"My name is Malorie, and I don't have an accent."

"To me, you do. A very nice one."

"Then you must love it around here, where everybody talks like me."

"I'm starting to like it more each day."

Malorie looked away and focused on eating the sundae before it melted. Later, she would lament the fact that the sundae had been completely wasted calories. She couldn't taste anything with a handsome man like Sacha Mikhelson flirting so openly with her. She was surprised she was getting the ice cream into her mouth and not spilling it down her shirt like a toddler at a birthday party.

They arrived at the park, where they let the dogs off their leashes within the enclosed space that was reserved for small dogs. Malorie and Sacha stood watching as the two brown pooches rolled and cavorted on the grass.

Sacha Mikhelson said, "Our dogs have royal names. Princess and Duke. What do you suppose that makes us?"

She turned to him and said firmly, "Friends, Sacha. It makes us just friends."

"I meant..."

"I know what you meant," she said. "But, before you waste all your Russian charm on me, you should know something. I'm not single."

"But you are not married. Not yet."

"Not for lack of trying." She let out an awkward laugh.

He didn't smile, let alone laugh.

"I'm working on it," she said.

"For someone who claims to be working on it, I can't help but notice there are two things missing," he said. "There is no engagement ring on your finger, and there is no happiness in your eyes."

"I'm probably still jet lagged," she said. "Don't worry about me. I'm happy. I have a great job and an amazing dog, and life is good."

"If that is true, then I am very happy for you." He offered his hand. "I am always happy for my friends."

"Friends," she agreed and shook his hand. "And I'm Malorie." She frowned. Hadn't she already said her name? The Russian was making her repeat herself.

"I did not forget," he said. "I never forget the names of my enemies or my friends."

Malorie turned away from the Russian's gaze and called for the dogs, who were getting a little far away for her liking. Princess came bounding back, Duke right behind her in hot pursuit. Just like a man! He caught up, and they tumbled in a ball of brown fur.

"This is nice," Malorie said. "There are a lot of dogs in the neighborhood, but most of them are too big to play with Princess. I'm glad we were able to get through our misunderstanding and become friends." She glanced up at his profile, which was as perfect and handsome as his face was from the front. Better even, because those icy-blue eyes weren't making her lose her short term memory and repeat herself.

"Mmm," he said, enigmatically.

"Don't tell me you're one of those guys who can't be friends with a woman."

"I have many women friends." He grinned.

She turned away. "I bet you do."

Chapter 16

A funny thing happened Saturday.

Or, rather, didn't happen.

Malorie Meyers didn't go by Lars's custom stereo shop and try to ambush the man who'd left her at the altar with no explanation. Instead, she cleaned the apartment from top to bottom, setting aside a pile of the personal things he'd left behind. She considered chucking everything in the garbage but didn't. If Lars was too good for a stick of deodorant that still had twenty percent of its contents, that was between him and the environment.

That night, Malorie took Princess for her walk a little earlier than the time that had been their habit the past six days. They left the apartment at ten o'clock. Woman and dog arrived at the off-leash, small-dogs-only portion of the park just as Sacha was leaving with Duke.

Sacha said, "Hello, friend. Tomorrow night, I come later. Good night." He gave her a quick nod and was on his way.

"Sounds good. Have a great night," Malorie called after him.

And that was it.

The dogs had interacted for longer than the humans.

Malorie played the entire conversation—all fifteen words—over and over in her head. *Hello, friend. Tomorrow night, I come later. Good night.* Then, *sounds good. Have a great night.*

The brief exchange was like a song she couldn't get out of her head. It continued playing through her dreams as she slept, with Princess by her side.

A note about the sleeping arrangements: Malorie had dutifully read up on the care and training of small dogs. She was still no expert, but she was a conscientious person in general, and she'd educated herself. That was why there was a small dog bed on the floor, next to the bed. It would help Princess to remember her place within the pack, which was not at the top of the social hierarchy. This would help prevent behavioral issues down the road.

However, Princess had learned about humans. Not through an internet search or book from the library but through life experience. She knew that as soon as the human's breathing pattern changed, she could leave the subpar temporary bed, way down on the floor, and jump up to where she belonged, on the Big Bed. When the human's breathing changed again in the morning, she would jump down again, settle in the subpar location way down on the floor, and wait for the Good Words of Praise.

* * *

On Sunday night, Malorie arrived at the park at the same time as Sacha and Duke.

"Hello, friend," she said.

"Hello," he said. "No stars tonight."

"It was cloudy all day," she said.

They unleashed the dogs, who tumbled and sniffed each other while making happy snorts and yips.

They watched the dogs play for fifteen minutes without speaking.

Then Sacha whistled for Duke, attached the dog's leash, and said, "Good night." He walked away briskly, not waiting for her.

* * *

On Monday night, Sacha said, "Stars tonight."

"The sky was clear all day," Malorie said.

They looked up at the stars, watched the dogs play, and then Sacha said good night.

Malorie checked the time on her phone. Seventeen minutes had passed. Sunday night, it had been fifteen.

* * *

On Tuesday night, it was raining.

"Rain," Sacha said.

"No stars," Malorie said.

They stood in the rain, watching the dogs, for twenty minutes before Sacha left.

* * *

On Wednesday night, it was warm but cloudy.

You get the picture.

* * *

On Friday night, Malorie said, out of the blue, "I'm painting my apartment."

"When?"

"Tomorrow," she said. "I get weekends off, and I like to stay busy. I'll start tomorrow morning, and if I don't get it all done, I still have Sunday."

"Painting is a big job," Sacha said. "Give me your address."

"Oh, I was just making conversation. I wasn't fishing for any free labor. Honestly."

"I help," he said, laying on the thick Russian accent. "You take my help or I am offended, yes?"

"I guess the dogs could have a play date," she said.

"Sure." He handed her his phone with an open contact card for herself. It read: *Malorie, 10:10 pm Dog Park, Friend.*

Malorie punched in her apartment address and the buzzer number for the intercom.

"I was thinking of starting around ten or eleven o'clock," she said.

"Do you have paint?"

"Not yet, but there's a paint store nearby."

"Eleven o'clock is too late. Ten o'clock is also too late. I will be there at eight."

"That's less than ten hours from right now," she said. "It doesn't give me much time to clean up the apartment and hide all the bloodstains."

Sacha grinned. "We paint over bloodstains. We use good primer."

Chapter 17

Saturday

Malorie Meyers had barely slept at all Friday night. She'd noticed, for the first time, her Chihuahua's habit of sneaking onto the bed. Malorie pretended not to have noticed. The dog pretended not to have noticed the human pretending to not notice.

Princess was on her dog bed on the floor in the morning, so Malorie gave her the Good Words of Praise, even though both of them knew it was a farce.

Malorie jumped out of bed and did some last-minute tidying. She grabbed the big cardboard box full of Lars's things and brought it down to the storage locker in the basement. As she was cramming the box in between the Christmas decorations and mystery boxes covered in dust, the landlord came in, carrying some tools. He owned the building, but he was an active landlord, acting also as the handyman.

"You're up early," said the landlord, an elderly Scottish man named Doug. "Can't wait to get painting, can you?"

"A friend is coming by to help, and my friend thought ten or eleven was too late. Thanks, by the way, for giving me permission to paint the place. You really are the best landlord."

Doug said gruffly, "Butter me up with flattery all you want, Missy, but if I hear any complaints about your dog barking, both of you are out of here." Then, once the landlord business was out of the way, he said in a softer tone, "I really am sorry about what happened with you and Lars. When he comes back, I hope he likes the new paint color."

"What makes you think he's coming back?"

"Lars always comes back," Doug said. "Why wouldn't he this time?"

"Maybe I won't let him."

"You always say that."

"No, I don't."

With a sniff, Doug said lightly, "Okay." He put the tools away in the tool locker then brushed the dust off his hands. "Good luck painting today. Don't paint over the electrical outlet covers."

"Who would paint over the outlet covers?"

"Don't get me started," he said.

She held up one hand as though swearing an oath in court. "I promise to carefully remove all of the outlet covers before I paint the walls."

"Just the walls," he said, waving a crooked finger. "Don't paint the countertops, the floors, or the toilet."

"Who would paint a toilet?"

"Don't get me started," he said again.

"You've been at this business a long time. You probably know people better than they know themselves."

"You might say that." He turned to leave but paused. "You can keep the gift card for the steak house. That's for you, even if you don't get back with Lars right away. Use it to treat the girlfriend who's coming to help you paint."

"It's not a girlfriend," Malorie said. "It's a man. We met at the dog park. He has a Chihuahua, so the dogs are going to have a play date while we paint."

Doug raised his eyebrows and gave her a long, silent look. Then he said, "Keep those dogs quiet," and left.

Malorie finished stuffing things into her locker, realized it was almost eight o'clock already, and ran back to her apartment at top speed.

The intercom was buzzing when Malorie walked in the door. Princess was barking at the intercom, which she hadn't heard yet and was clearly alarmed by.

Malorie buzzed in Sacha, then spent the next minute trying to convince the Chihuahua that the intercom was not the devil coming to make hot dogs out of tiny dogs.

What Malorie forgot to do, thanks to the visit with Doug in the storage room and the yapping, was put away one thing. One big, white, fluffy thing. Her wedding dress. The one she'd gotten back from the cleaners on Tuesday and left in the middle of her closet.

As Malorie had looked at the dress, she'd imagined it had a life of its own. Dreams of its own. She closed the closet doors, but that wasn't enough.

Malorie had a paranoid thought that her closet doors might suddenly fly open of their own accord, and then Sacha would see the dress, and then it would be a Whole Big Thing.

Hiding the dress was a good idea, except she hadn't figured out where to hide it.

Inside the oven was a good contender, which was why the plastic garment bag was on top of the stove when Malorie opened the apartment door.

"Good morning," Sacha said. He was holding a cardboard tray with four hot beverage containers from his ice cream shop. "I don't know what you drink, so I brought an assortment."

"Come in," she said.

Duke was already inside, sniffing the shoes by the door.

Sacha leaned forward, glanced around, then leaned back again. He didn't come inside.

"I've seen enough," he said. "I know the perfect color. Let's go. The paint store has been open for half an hour already."

"You know the perfect color? But I've already picked a color. I have the samples right here." She showed him a handful of swatches. All had been preapproved by Doug, but she was having a tough time choosing between two off-white shades.

Sacha plucked from her hand the swatch that Doug hadn't been as keen on. It was a pale pastel, like the others, but midway between a buttery yellow and warm peach.

"This one," Sacha said. He held it next to her face and furrowed his brow. "Yes. This is the one."

"People don't pick paint to match themselves," she said.

"Why not?"

She was genuinely stumped. Why didn't people pick paint colors to match themselves?

Sacha called for Duke, who came to his feet obediently. Princess did as well.

Malorie grabbed her purse and jacket. After a few minutes of deliberating over which Butter Spoons beverage she wanted and then leaving the extras on the coffee table at the apartment, they left for the paint store.

At the paint store, Sacha was quick and efficient in helping Malorie choose the paint finish and calculate the amount needed for the small, two-bedroom apartment.

Everything was going well until they hit a hitch.

The young man ringing up the order asked for Malorie's keys.

"Why?" She looked from the young man to Sacha, who was barely concealing a smirk. "You don't need to measure my walls or anything. Worst-case scenario, I'll come back and get another bucket or two."

The young man said, "We can't send the painting crew in unless we have access. If you want to stick around and let the guys in yourself, they should be packed up in twenty minutes." He looked at Sacha. "It's today you wanted the job done, isn't it? Did I mess up?"

"You have not messed up," Sacha said. "It's today. You will have it done by what time?"

"The paint dries quickly, so we'll be able to finish up by four o'clock, maybe five at the latest."

Malorie ask the clerk for a moment, then said to Sacha, "We've had another one of our funny misunderstandings. I'm not paying to have them paint my apartment."

"Do you have a ladder?"

"No, but I'm sure the landlord has one I can borrow. Or I'll just stand on a chair."

Sacha said to the clerk, "Is it safe to stand on a chair while painting?"

The clerk winced. "We don't recommend it."

"And your crew is trained and comes with insurance?"

"Absolutely," the clerk said. "Every job comes with our Trouble-Free Guarantee."

Sacha said to Malorie, "This company did the paint at Butter Spoons. It was trouble free." He nodded at the clerk and raised his eyebrows expectantly at Malorie. "Give him your keys." He raised one finger. "And don't worry about the cost. I have it covered."

"I can't let you pay for my paint job."

"Why not? I said I would help. This is me, helping."

Malorie glanced out the window to check on the dogs. Duke and Princess were enjoying some attention from a family that had been passing by.

Malorie handed her keys to the clerk. "Tell them to wiggle the one for the deadbolt. It's a bit sticky."

"Fix that, please," Sacha said, then he named a compound for lubricating locks without making them gummy. "I trust you have that in stock?"

"We do," the clerk said, typing something into the computer. "It will be as good as new." He clicked his mouse, and the printer started whirring. "Everything's set up. You just need to be back here before we close at six o'clock so you can get your keys back."

"Off to our next stop," Sacha said brightly.

Malorie walked away from the counter—and her apartment keys—very slowly. Why did she feel like she'd been blindsided?

Because she had been.

That was why.

And yet there was a part of her that wasn't surprised at all.

She barely knew Sacha Mikhelson, and yet some part of her knew that Sacha volunteering to help and then hiring a painting crew was *exactly* what he'd always been going to do. Just like how she'd known that Doug, the landlord, would let her keep Princess. Malorie had her blind spots, but she was learning.

Oh, the look on Lars Lundin's face when he found out a Russian had paid to repaint their apartment! It was going to be priceless.

Chapter 18

Malorie Meyers didn't hate the idea of people working in her apartment while she was out. She wondered if that was how Penny felt at Penntastic whenever she dropped a pile of work on Malorie's desk and went for a long "lunch," coming back three hours later with a new handbag and a fresh manicure.

Malorie and Sacha left the paint store and gathered the dogs. Sacha opened the back door of a sporty convertible that was parked in front of the paint store. Duke hopped in and settled on a folded towel in the back seat.

Malorie hadn't realized Sacha's car was there, since they'd walked to the paint store from her apartment. He must have left it there when he stopped in at opening time to set up the painting job. All the better to surprise her.

There was a second folded towel in the back seat. Princess walked over it and sat on the towel next to Duke. Well, she basically sat right on top of him, but he wriggled over to make room.

"Those two," Sacha said of the dogs. "Can you believe it? They get along so well. They must have known each other in another life."

"Dogs are much simpler than people," she said.

"People can be simple," Sacha said. "If you allow them to be."

He opened the passenger door and waved for her to get in.

"Nice wheels," she said.

"I know," he said. "That's why I picked this one. And the car isn't bad, either."

Sacha climbed in, donned some aviator sunglasses, revved the engine, and pulled out onto the road.

The day was gorgeous—warm, but with enough cloud cover that Malorie wasn't dying for air conditioning. The sporty convertible turned heads. Malorie felt like a celebrity with all the attention.

She stared at Sacha while he was driving, noting that his temples were flecked with a smattering of gray. His eyes had some small lines at the edges, even when he wasn't grinning. She wondered how old he actually was. The dimples made him look twenty-five, but the gray said otherwise.

She asked, "What year did your family move here?"

"I'm forty-one," he said with a chuckle. "That is what you're trying to figure out, is it not?"

"You got me. I'm not very subtle."

"If there's something you want to know, ask. People can be simple."

"Like dogs," she said.

"Like dogs," he agreed.

"Except without as much sniffing."

He shrugged. "I don't mind."

"Where are you taking us?"

"Does it matter? You were going to be painting your apartment all day. I know you don't have anywhere you need to be."

"I guess I'm all yours for the day. You paid for it."

He lowered his sunglasses and gave her an amused look.

"That's not how I meant it," she said.

He sniffed. "People say what they mean, especially when they say they aren't."

"Fine. I'm your paid escort for the day. Your high-end call girl."

"Eh," he said, bobbing his head to the side. "The paint job wasn't that much."

"How would you know how much a full day with a high-end call girl costs?"

He chuckled. "Where do you want to go first? Shopping? More coffee?"

"I could eat," she said. "If you turn around and go back to Baker Street, we could try Delilah's. It's still early, so the line for brunch shouldn't be that long."

"I do not wait in lines," he said.

Tentatively, she asked, "Is that a Russian thing?"

He scoffed. "It is an impatience thing."

"You're impatient?" She smirked. "Wow. I hadn't noticed by how you showed up five minutes early and then stood at the doorway tapping your toe like I was late."

"Patience is for young people," he said. "I'm forty-one. I don't leave decisions open." He waved at the road ahead. "I haven't been to the Pier. I hear it's a place I must see."

"If you don't like waiting in lines, you're not going to like the Pier. It's fun, but it is tourist central this time of year."

"The lines won't be so bad," he said. "Not if I have company. Thank you for coming with me today. I have been lonely, and it is good to have company. I know that is not very Russian to say, and I apologize for not being a Russian stereotype, but I have been living here for some time."

Malorie was speechless. Had Sacha just said he was lonely? Who admitted something like that? It was like confessing to being deeply in debt or worse.

They drove to the Pier. It was still early, so the lineups didn't look nearly as bad as Malorie had expected—at first glance, anyway. They parked in a great spot, gathered the dogs, and went in search of breakfast.

Getting up early on Saturday clearly had an upside. Ordinarily, she and Lars would be lounging around in pajamas at this time of day. Then he would pop down to the stereo shop for some work, and she would find some way to busy herself in the apartment until he got home. She wouldn't hang out with her girlfriends because she didn't have any. Her parents were deceased, and she had no siblings. Doug, the Scottish landlord she'd been renting from for the last decade, was the closest thing to family she had. The only reason Doug hadn't been there, at the wedding-that-didn't-happen, was because he had another wedding out of town, for his actual daughter.

Lars and his friends were Malorie's entire social circle. That was why Malorie had asked her boss, Penny, and Yuki Noguchi to be her maid of honor and bridesmaid, respectively. Malorie had worked for Penny for years, so it seemed logical. Malorie didn't know Yuki that well, but the young woman was always asking questions about the wedding plans, so it seemed logical to give her an active role. Yuki was so helpful, too. She was always volunteering to check with Lars about everything from wedding cake flavors to the colors of flowers on the tables.

Chapter 19

Sacha reluctantly allowed Malorie to pay for breakfast.

"It's only fair," she said.

"With men and women, there is no such thing as fair," he said. "Not since the beginning of time. It has never been fair."

"Is that a Russian thing? We do things differently around here."

"So you say."

After breakfast, Malorie found some handmade pottery that perfectly matched the paint chip in her pocket. She was only going to buy one mug, because they weren't cheap, but Sacha frowned with disapproval until she picked up another one so she'd have a matching pair.

Malorie didn't usually buy much stuff, especially not tourist-oriented stuff she didn't need, but it was so much fun to hold things up and see if Sacha disapproved—frowning face—or approved—neutral expression.

At the end of the day, after a second meal and a lot of walking, the trunk of the convertible was full of souvenirs and artwork. Sacha had picked up some framed prints from a local artist. He bought six of the same print, "for family," he'd said.

As they got into the car to return to the paint shop before it closed, Malorie was surprised at how quickly and enjoyably the day had gone by. Sacha, despite claiming to have no patience, seemed to actually enjoy walking and window-shopping. He hadn't pulled out his phone or checked the time once.

If Melanie had been there with Lars, he would have regarded the entire day as a personal favor to Malorie, for which she would owe him.

On the drive back, she asked, "So, why here? Why not open your Butter Spoons test location in one of the bigger cities?"

Sacha said, "We have other test locations. They are all running right now."

"But you're here all the time? Who's running the other ones?"

With his fake thick accent, he said, "Crazy Russian man can bark orders over phone. Crazy Russian man hear the fear in voice. He knows staff do good job. Staff do good job, or else." He mimed cutting a throat.

"I had some crazy bosses when I was a teenager," Malorie said. "You're making me wonder how much of it was an act."

"Who can say?" In his regular accent, he said, "What about you? Why aren't you in New York or Los Angeles, working in the fashion industry there? Or Europe?"

She laughed and then stopped, perplexed. Why, indeed? "I don't know," she said.

Up until recently, the answer had been because Lars would never want to move. His family lived here, and his business was established. He never wanted to leave.

Malorie loved the city and her job, but she didn't know if it was only because she was sensible, making the most of what she had. Would the love last in some alternate future where she had other options?

"It is good city," Sacha said with the exaggerated accent. "We paint apartment. Make nice. You stay. We go to dog park every night at ten after ten." He turned to her and added, "We are friends."

"We are friends," she agreed. "And I like the sound of that. Nothing beats a routine if it's a good one."

Chapter 20

Sacha pulled out his phone for the first time that day. It was five thirty, and he had just parked his car in front of the paint store, in the exact same spot he'd been parked before their excursion.

He looked at the screen, frowned, and said, "I have to take care of something at the store."

"Anything I can help with?"

"No," he said emphatically. "Go inside and get your keys before they close. The paint job was not that expensive, but a hotel night for you at the last minute would add to the bill."

"I wouldn't expect you to pay for a hotel for me."

"Where else would you stay?" His question was serious, not flirtatious. Malorie wondered if he had figured out she had very few people she could count on in the city. She had no family, no friends that weren't Lars's friends, and nowhere to crash on a couch if an emergency came up. Had Sacha figured it out by her lack of mentioning other people in conversation? She might have mentioned the work colleague, Yuki, who had become closer, but that would have meant bringing up Yuki's role as bridesmaid in the wedding-that-didn't-happen, and Malorie didn't want to do that. It was bad enough getting questions and sad looks from people who knew. She didn't want her new friendship with Sacha Mikhelson to be tainted by her status as a loser, a lonely woman who'd been left at the altar.

"Don't worry about where I'll stay tonight," she said. "It's not going to be an issue. The paint shop doesn't close for another half hour."

He glanced up from his phone. "Twenty-eight minutes," he said.

"I'm going, I'm going," she said hurriedly.

Malorie said goodbye to Duke, unglued Princess from her buddy, got out of the convertible, and stood on the sidewalk. She felt like she was forgetting something. What? Her head was swimming from all the excitement of the day, plus the sunshine. She hadn't spent an entire summer day outside since she was a kid. Most Saturdays involved a lot more indoor time.

Sacha was back frowning at his phone, typing a response.

"Thank you for everything," she said.

"You're welcome," he said, glancing up briefly before returning his attention to his phone. "Forgive me, but I may not be at the usual place tonight at ten past ten."

"You won't?"

"Not tonight. I hope the apartment paint meets your standards. If not, you tell me, and I will tell them."

"I'm sure it will be fine," she said.

He gave her a quick nod, then pulled away in the car.

Princess, who was in Malorie's arms, licked her owner's face.

"Thanks *so* much," Malorie said. "I was just thinking that all this date needed was some tongue kissing at the end. Maybe not from someone with doggy breath, but I appreciate the sentiment."

Malorie stayed on the sidewalk a few minutes. She had forgotten something, she was sure of it. Plus she had the strangest idea Sacha had been kidding about needing to leave and would be back in a minute after circling the block.

But he didn't roll up, and the paint store was closing soon.

Malorie went inside, gathered her keys, thanked the staff, and walked back to her place.

When Malorie walked into her apartment, she thought for an instant she'd walked into the wrong place. The walls weren't just brighter and fresher; they practically glowed. The apartment's windows were an adequate size, but they weren't exactly wall-to-wall. The new paint color, however, caught every ray of early-evening sunshine.

The tiny space looked larger and newer, and it didn't even reek of chemicals. The paint store hadn't been joking about their premium formulation being quick drying and low VOC. Even with the windows closed, she could barely smell a hint of it.

The crew had put all of Malorie's furniture back in different places. Not wrong, but different.

Now everything was oriented to the sunny picture window instead of pointing at the spot where Lars had insisted on hanging an overly large television. The new layout looked incredible. Malorie was a little embarrassed she hadn't figured out that furniture arrangement herself.

Princess hopped up on the couch, unperturbed by it being at a different angle, and settled down for a snooze. She'd had a big day walking around and getting attention from strangers. A single cute Chihuahua attracted a decent number of people. Two of them together attracted four times as many. During their walks along the crowded boardwalk, Malorie and Sacha had joked about being the entourage for a pair of celebrity dogs. It was one of many shared jokes they'd enjoyed all day.

Malorie settled on the couch next to Princess, taking in the new view. The apartment was on the third floor, looking over the rooftops of houses. The dog park was visible in the distance.

A big vase of flowers sat on the living room coffee table. The card was from Gardenia Flowers, down the street. The arrangement was mostly cheap and cheerful daisies, a cute finishing touch from the painting crew that couldn't have cost much. Even so, they brought life to the space, which was exactly what the place had needed.

The only thing that would have made coming home better would have been coming home with a companion. Besides Princess.

Malorie pulled out her phone and sent a message to Lars with a picture of the freshly painted apartment. No text, just the picture. He would understand immediately. He'd been talking about painting the apartment for the last two or three years, but they kept putting it off until "after the wedding." They'd put off a lot of things until "after the wedding," such as the discussion about starting a family. Even simple decisions like upgrading the coffee maker had been put off until "after the wedding."

Malorie's phone vibrated with an incoming message.

Lars: *The old place looks great.*

Malorie's heart pounded so hard it made her head rattle.

It was the first response she'd gotten from Lars since the wedding-that-didn't-happen.

She wanted to write back a long message but stopped herself. Lars could spook easily. She waited a full five minutes, then sent a photo of the paint sample card with the name visible. The paint was called Passion Pastel #5.

Lars: *Good choice.*

Malorie couldn't decide what to send a photo of next. She accidentally sent a blurry one of her foot.

Lars: *I can't really chat right now. We should catch up soon.*

Malorie played it cool and sent the thumbs-up emoticon.

She spent the rest of the evening making an extremely complicated personal-sized pizza. She ate it while watching television from the only seat that faced it directly—a chair she hadn't realized was very comfortable.

She took Princess for a walk at the usual time. She hoped Sacha would be there, despite his warning that he might not make it. He didn't show up.

She wondered if she had done something wrong that day.

Had she offended him with all the teasing about his Russian ways?

Should she have tried harder to pay him back for the paint job? She'd had to fight to get him to let her pay for some of their food that day. Sacha didn't seem worried about money.

How could she pay him back for his kindness? All the things she knew about paying guys back for favors were not appropriate for a man and woman who were only friends.

Malorie walked home the long way, avoiding Butter Spoons in case Sacha was still there working after hours. She didn't want him to see her peering in the window like a stalker.

As she climbed into bed that night, she realized what she'd forgotten when they'd returned to the paint store. All of her treasures—the day's purchases at the Pier—were still in the trunk of Sacha's car.

Knowing that her things were safely with him made her smile as she fell asleep.

What Malorie hadn't noticed, and didn't think about that night, was the big, white wedding dress.

It hadn't been in the kitchen when she'd gotten home, but who notices the absence of something that shouldn't have been there in the first place? She hadn't even given it a second thought when she'd turned on the oven for her pizza—which was exactly why it would have been a stupid idea for her to stash it in there.

Not only was the freshly cleaned wedding dress not in the kitchen, it wasn't in the apartment at all.

It would take some time for Malorie to realize the dress was missing.

For now, she enjoyed the pleasant dreams a person got to have at the end of a very good day.

Chapter 21

Saturday Night

Lars Lundin

Lars kept pulling out his phone and looking at the last text messages from Malorie. Why had she sent him a picture of her foot? Was it something sexual? Had she gotten into some new, weird stuff since the last time they'd been together?

He couldn't put it out of his head.

Why a blurry photo of her foot? Why not some other body part? Was she playing hard to get?

It wasn't like Malorie to drive him mad with unanswered questions like that. Usually, she was so up front and honest about everything that he hardly ever had to try reading between the lines.

Yuki Noguchi, however, was the complete opposite.

Rather than simply tell Lars to never put her special tea mugs in the dishwasher, she would find them in the top rack, remove them without saying anything, and then passive-aggressively wash them very loudly in the sink. While clearing her throat.

Lars hadn't figured out what the mug thing was all about. All he knew was that whenever he tried to help out around the condo, he got in trouble. Any time he touched something, he was warned that it was fragile and irreplaceable.

"Your vacuum cleaner isn't that special," he'd say. "I could go down to the secondhand shop and get a dozen vacuum cleaners exactly like this!"

"You would not," she'd say. "It's an import. You can't even buy bags for it here. That's why I always sweep first before I vacuum, so the bag doesn't fill up."

Lars would start to lose his cool. "What's the point in having a vacuum cleaner if you have to sweep first?"

"Do I have to explain everything to you like you're a child?"

"Yes. Explain it to me like I'm five."

Then Yuki would find something about Lars losing his cool to be attractive. He was a very handsome man, so it wasn't that difficult.

"My big, silly Viking man," she would say.

Then she would give him one of her adorably coy flirtatious looks. He would take her in his arms, and the fight would be over.

Until the next time Lars used the shower in a careless fashion or touched the vacuum cleaner or put her precious mugs in the dishwasher.

Chapter 22

Sunday

Malorie Meyers

Malorie woke up early on Sunday. She'd expected to sleep in late after the full day she'd enjoyed on Saturday, but she wasn't tired at all.

She rolled over and greeted Princess, who was pretending she'd just woken up on her dog bed.

"You little liar," Malorie said.

Princess wagged her tail, even though she didn't like that word.

"There's a warm spot right here beside me," Malorie said. "You and I both know you were sleeping next to me all night."

Princess batted her short eyelashes innocently. Why was the human so obsessed with the Big Bed? Or warm spots, for that matter? Who didn't love a warm spot? Clearly there was some sort of quirk in the apartment's heating and cooling system that caused a warm spot to randomly manifest on the Big Bed. It was not anything to be concerned about.

Malorie got up, showered, and had breakfast.

As she was putting her cereal bowl in the dishwasher, her phone alerted her to a new message.

Was it Lars, begging to come home?

No.

It was a message from an unknown number: *I have something of yours.*

Malorie's heart skipped a beat. Who would send her such a menacing message? Was a ransom note coming next?

A second message came in from the same number: *This is Sacha.*

She laughed out loud in relief. She had put her phone number into his contact list when she'd given him her address on Friday night. Now, thanks to this text, she had his number, too. That would be handy if they didn't see each other at the dog park for a while and she got worried about her friend.

Malorie wrote back: *You have all my treasures from the Pier. I left them in your trunk.*

Sacha: *Your mistake. Now I am holding them for ransom.*

Malorie: *Name your price.*

There was a delay on his reply.

"No, really," she said out loud to her phone. "Tell me how I can repay you for being such a great friend."

Sacha: *Come by the ice cream shop today and be difficult. Wear the sweatshirt.*

Malorie: *What are you talking about?*

Sacha: *I'm training the staff to deal with trouble customers. Come in and yell at them.*

Malorie: *They seem like nice kids. I don't know if I'll be able to yell at them.*

Sacha: *At least come in and try some of the new toppings. I will be here all day.*

She replied that she would drop by after she took care of a few things.

She turned on the dishwasher. That pretty much took care of her chores for the day. She'd already cleaned the apartment in preparation for painting.

She turned on the television to kill an hour or two before heading down to Butter Spoons.

Thirty-seven minutes into watching nothing, she clicked it off and headed out with Princess.

When she got to Butter Spoons, the trio of staff were working diligently. Or so it appeared from her view through the front window, from outside of the shop. Word must have gotten out about the place. There was a lineup longer than the one that formed in front of Delilah's on the weekend. Malorie couldn't get anywhere near the door, let alone inside. Not any time soon.

It was too bad she wouldn't get to play the role of Difficult Customer. She'd already formulated an acting script. She was going to walk in with her dog then pitch an entitled fit when the staff asked her to leave the pet outside. She probably would have broken character and started giggling, but it might have been fun for a minute or two. She could have channeled Shawn's ex, Sharise. What a character that woman was!

Behind her, a man with a Texan drawl said, "I don't know what the big line is all about. People can get ice cream anywhere."

"But not like this," she said. "Butter Spoons has..." She turned around to find Sacha standing behind her, an amused expression on his face.

He said, still in the Texan drawl, "Yes? Butter Spoons has what? Sell me on it, ma'am."

"I knew it was you," she said, because on some level, she had. But how? Had she smelled him? Was she picking up smelling superpowers from her Chihuahua?

"You did not suspect a thing," he said.

"Your bad accent was a dead giveaway."

He dropped his gaze from her eyes to her clothes. "You didn't wear the big sweatshirt."

"That's only for late-night trips to the Quick Stop, when I need to look unhinged. That's my prime time for extorting cash out of people with dogs."

"I knew it," he said. "I knew you weren't a fashion designer. That's not a real job. It's something people on TV pretend to do."

"I told you yesterday, I'm more of an administrative assistant for my boss, Penny."

"Penny is a lucky woman to have you." His icy-blue eyes were unwavering, communicating more than his words.

Malorie had to look away. It was not the sort of look friends gave each other.

"I should collect my stuff from your trunk and let you get back to work," she said.

"Why do you think I would go back to work?"

She glanced at the lineup, which was only getting longer, then back at those captivating eyes.

"Because it's busy," she said. "And only getting busier."

"Exactly," he said. "I'm the CEO. My job is to make it get busy. It's the employees' jobs to serve the ice cream. As you can see, my job is done for the day."

"You don't like scooping ice cream and talking to strangers?"

"Why would I talk to strangers when I could spend the day relaxing with a friend?"

"Do you mean me? That's presumptive of you. I might have big plans for the day."

"Yesterday, there were four people painting your apartment. You knew that, doing it yourself, it would take you at least two days. You did not make plans with your friends today."

"You got me," she said, laughing. "Also, I don't have any friends."

He frowned. "You don't?"

"That was a joke," she said. Mostly a joke.

"You have me now," he said. "What other places in this city do I need to see?" He leaned down and greeted Princess. "Dog-friendly places," he added.

"I'll have to think about it," she said. "I know the place, but I haven't been anyone's tour guide in a really long time." Not since Lars Lundin had moved to the city and swept Malorie off her feet twelve years ago.

Sacha said, "You think about it while I go inside to get Duke."

He pushed his way through the crowd, back into Butter Spoons.

The aroma of vanilla wafted out of the building. Some of the people who'd been in line for Delilah's switched lines and came over to the line for the ice cream shop.

Malorie did a mental checklist of all the places she'd taken Lars during the early days of their relationship. They had been to museums, art galleries, garden parks, outdoor concerts, natural features, historical landmarks, and locations that had been used for film and TV.

Where to start?

She knew almost immediately. They would start with the garden park then visit the Russian Tea Room. It was nothing like the famous one in New York. The local Russian Tea Room was much more casual, the perfect place to enjoy a quiet moment after touring the park's luscious greenery and flowers.

Chapter 23

Monday

Malorie slid the new, smaller bed under her desk at work. Princess hopped on it hesitantly.

Princess couldn't understand the human's obsession with beds and the size and location of beds. A bed was a bed, and bigger was better. This bed smelled like the inside of a store, and it was small.

Princess did a test circle then two more circles before falling onto her side. To her surprise, the bed wasn't too small after all. It was comfortable. It was just right!

She barked once to let the human know that a good job had been done. Humans needed to be given a lot of reassurance.

"You're welcome," Malorie said.

Malorie picked up the massive borrowed dog bed and lugged it back to Pedro the Labradoodle, care of Paul.

She had to turn sideways to get the giant thing through the accountant's doorway.

"Let me help you with that," Paul said, jumping up gallantly. He also spilled a mug of coffee all over himself not so gallantly.

"I got it," Malorie said, plopping the dog bed next to the couch where Pedro was currently stretched out. "At ease, soldier," she said to the accountant.

Paul looked down at himself. "Aww, shoot. I spilled coffee all over my new sweater vest." He looked further down. "And my pants. And my favorite argyle socks. Darn it. These are the ones Yuki said were sexy."

"Did she?" Malorie tilted her head. Paul did have a tendency to read a lot more into the casual things Yuki said than a nonlovesick person might.

Paul pulled off the sweater vest, revealing a white shirt with sweat stains plus a giant brown coffee stain.

"I think the vest is better," Malorie said. "The big diamonds hide the stain."

"It's argyle," Paul said, adding a tsk-tsk. "As a fashion designer, you should know better than to refer to argyle as merely diamonds."

"We both know I'm more of an assistant than a designer."

"What matters is what's printed on your business card. That's why I'm the chief financial officer."

"That you are," she said. "Did you have a good weekend?"

"I took Pedro to the groomer's. He had a *great* weekend. He's a pretty boy now."

Malorie looked over at the couch, at the large dog with the brown curls. Pedro looked the same as he'd been the week before. Shaggy. His furry eyebrows were hanging over his eyes. If Paul had been her friend and not just her work buddy, she might have questioned the groomer's abilities.

Paul dabbed at his shirt with the dry corner of his sweater vest. "What about you, Malorie? Did you get around to painting your apartment? I've really got to paint my condo one of these days. It's such a big job."

"It doesn't have to be," she said. "I had a paint crew come in. They did it all on Saturday."

"Wow. Look at you, delegating like a boss. What did you do? Sit on the couch and watch?"

"I went out. I was at the Pier all day."

Paul stopped dabbing. "You were at the Pier? That's so funny. Pedro and I walk through there every Saturday, doing our usual rounds. I thought I saw you there, but then I saw the guy you were with, and he wasn't Lars, so I didn't think it was you."

"It wasn't Lars," she said. "It was my new friend. Sacha."

"Huh," Paul said. His phone started ringing. "Duty calls," he said wearily.

Malorie wanted to talk to Paul a little more about Sacha, reliving the experience by sharing it with another person. She lingered to see if the call was going to take long. Paul dropped into his chair heavily and stared up at the ceiling while the other person talked. It would be a long call after all.

She waved goodbye and went back to her desk.

A fresh pile of mail was waiting in the center of her desk. The mail carrier hadn't been there yet that day, but sometimes things came through the mail slot over the weekend. Malorie found she had absolutely no interest in ripping open the fat envelopes. Her shiny silver letter opener had lost its gleam.

Malorie pushed her chair back. Princess jumped out from under the desk, ready for action, shaking her body excitedly.

Malorie asked the dog, "Would you like a tour of the warehouse? You haven't been there yet."

The dog danced on her hind legs.

"I don't want to oversell it, but the warehouse can be fun," Malorie said. "Let's pick up a sample of the new menswear shirts in Paul's size so that Pedro's Big Daddy doesn't have to work in a wet shirt all day. Nobody likes a wet shirt, do they, Princess? No, they don't."

Malorie heard herself speaking in baby talk and immediately stopped, even though no one was around to hear it.

Did she talk to Princess that way around Sacha? She hoped not.

They had spent most of Sunday together, touring the city and walking with the dogs. There had been countless opportunities for Malorie to baby-talk one or both dogs. She decided she had probably not done it. She did have some dignity.

The truth was, Malorie had baby-talked to Princess six times on Sunday in front of Sacha. He had looked away out of embarrassment each time. But then he had baby-talked to Duke three times that day and twice to Princess, who wasn't even his dog, so he was not really one to judge.

Chapter 24

That Monday evening, Malorie met Sacha at the dog park at ten minutes after ten.

"We have stars tonight," he said. "A good end to a good day."

"How are things with the ice cream business?"

"Satisfactory," he said. "How was fashion design?"

"I gave the company's accountant a makeover," she said. "I wanted to cut his hair, but our boss pushed me out of the way and did it herself. It was a whole thing. We didn't get any work done at all."

"Your boss would not last for long at my company."

"Probably not. I'm not sure *I* would last."

He gave her a sly look. "You would last. I would make sure."

They turned toward the dogs and watched them playing.

After only ten minutes, Sacha called for Duke and wished Malorie a good night.

Malorie was surprised her friend was leaving so soon but didn't say anything.

She threw some toys for Princess until the Chihuahua was played out, then started walking toward home.

She didn't need anything at the Quick Stop but dropped in anyway because she could see that Justine was working that night.

"Hey, Justine. Is she okay to bring in like this?" Malorie pointed to Princess, who was by her heel.

"As long as she doesn't eat the Twinkies off the low shelf, she's fine by me," Justine said. "What's new with the crazy Russian?"

"We've done more than dog walking," Malorie said.

Justine's eyebrows went up. "Hang on." The store clerk grabbed two bags of popcorn, opened them both, and placed one on the counter in front of Malorie. The popcorn-sharing had started during the middle of the previous week, when Malorie had popped in with an update after one of her early doggy play dates with "the crazy Russian."

"Now talk," Justine said, tossing a handful of popcorn into her mouth. "Slowly, and with lots of details." Justine waggled her eyebrows. She had a glittering piercing in one eyebrow that picked up the light in the Quick Stop and sparkled. Justine was the same age as Malorie, which Malorie had been surprised to learn, though she couldn't say why. Perhaps it was that the idea of working in a convenience store at her age—night shifts in particular—was unsettling to Malorie. She had grown to like Justine and wanted something better for the woman.

"Don't get too excited," Malorie said. "It's not like we kissed or anything. We're just friends."

"No spoilers," Justine said. "Start at the beginning. I haven't seen you since Friday night, when you tricked the crazy Russian into painting your apartment. Did he show up?"

"He did. He showed up at my place with four kinds of coffee, and when we got to the paint store, I found out he hired a crew to do the paint job for us. I didn't even touch a paint roller."

"No way."

"He said it was his way of helping, and he'd be offended if I didn't accept his help."

Justine shook her head. "That man is crazy but in a good way." She loaded up more popcorn. "What color paint did you choose?"

Malorie showed her the sample, which she still had in her purse for no reason except that she enjoyed showing people. Planning to paint your apartment was a bit like planning a wedding. Other people liked to get involved, and Malorie liked that aspect.

"I called it," Justine said smugly. "That shade was my choice, too. So, what did you do after he sent a crew in to paint your apartment?"

"We went to the Pier."

"I love the Pier. I always buy the most useless crap there, but I love it."

Malorie told Justine about the day-long outing at the Pier and the sequel the next day.

Then Justine caught Malorie up on the details of Justine's complicated life. There were some unsavory aspects involving Justine's ex-husband and some custody issues with their ten-year-old-twins. However, it sounded like things were improving in general. Malorie felt fireworks of joy inside upon hearing each bit of good news in Justine's life. The woman had been through a lot, and she appreciated every good thing that came her way now.

No customers came into the store during their conversation.

Malorie and Justine were so caught up in the stories of their lives that neither of them noticed that Princess had noticed the Twinkies, which were on a low shelf at dog-chin height.

Princess couldn't understand why the shiny things smelled like food but also not like food. She bit into one of them to discover its secrets. A small amount of sugar spurted into her mouth. That was something!

She instantly knew that anything she liked this much would have to be forbidden. She didn't want to hear any of the Bad Words, so she very carefully picked up the bitten Twinkie and brought it around the corner of the shelf, where she wouldn't be seen by the humans.

Princess gingerly pulled away the shiny wrapper and ate the Intoxicatingly Good Thing inside. She wasn't sure she could finish it, but then she remembered she was not a quitter. She left the wrapper on the floor and crept around the display for a second one.

By then, however, the window of opportunity was closing.

The human she lived with was moving toward the door slowly, using the body language that meant she would be leaving soon, unless something happened with the voices and everything got more exciting than ever.

Justine was saying, "And he only hung out with you for ten minutes tonight? I don't get it. Was he tired? Did you see him yawning?"

"No, but I'm sure he's busy with the ice cream shop."

"Or maybe his girlfriend doesn't like him out too late on a weeknight."

"I don't think he has a girlfriend. He would have mentioned something like that."

"Then I guess that girl he comes in with sometimes must be his daughter." Justine looked down and rolled up the empty popcorn bag. "I don't know why I said that. No. That's not true. I said it because I thought you should know." She looked up and winced apologetically. "I should have told you sooner."

"He comes in with a girl? What does she look like?"

"Young. But not daughter-young."

Malorie shrugged. "It doesn't matter that he has a girlfriend. Good for him. It's much better than him thinking I'm leading him on."

"Good," Justine said. "I was worried you were going to get mad at me." She wrinkled her nose. "People tend to blame the messenger."

"I'm glad you told me."

Justine took in a big breath and said nothing.

In the silence, Malorie heard something near her feet. It was the unmistakable sound of a small dog experiencing gastrointestinal distress. She looked down at a very guilty-looking Chihuahua and asked the dog, "What did you do?"

What happened next was a bit of a blur.

"There's a Twinkie missing from the rack," Justine said. "That sneaky little brat!"

Malorie's vision went white with panic. Were Twinkies poisonous to dogs? They weren't exactly healthy for humans. Did she need to rush Princess to the vet? What about the wrapper? Where was the wrapper?

Justine came out from behind the counter and put a comforting arm across Malorie's shoulders. "Take a breath," she said. "Let's not panic. I see the wrapper on the floor by the cooler, and there's only one Twinkie missing. I know because I just restocked them. Princess is going to be okay."

"She is?"

"Yes. But you might want to lock her in the bathroom tonight with some old towels.

Another gurgle came out of the small dog. And a bad smell.

"I'm a bad mother," Malorie said, barely holding back the sobs. "A bad dog mother."

"We all make mistakes," Justine said. "I'm here for you, but, um, I'd be more comfortable if Princess wasn't inside my nice, clean store when the Twinkie takes effect."

Malorie apologized for her dog's behavior and tried to pay for the Twinkie and the popcorn, but Justine was very insistent about the two of them exiting the store.

They left, returning to the dog park.

Malorie spent the next three hours at the dog park, waiting for the end of the Twinkiepocalypse. She met other dog owners from the neighborhood who, upon hearing about the unfortunate event, told Malorie about the things their dogs had eaten. They must have thought they were cheering her up, but each tale was more horrifying than the last. There were so many everyday foods that were toxic to dogs— grapes, macadamia nuts, xylitol, garlic, and chocolate, to name a few—and then there was also a long list of foods, or even quantities, that could ruin a dog owner's day.

Eventually, Princess was empty and feeling much better.

Malorie walked home feeling paranoid about the future but relieved that the Twinkiepocalypse was over. She vowed to be more careful when visiting the Quick Stop from then on.

And she would be more careful, but Princess would become more cunning.

Princess had learned nothing from the adventure except that she liked eating Twinkies, no matter the cost.

The Chihuahua would enjoy another Twinkie soon.

Chapter 25

Tuesday

At work on Tuesday, Malorie told Paul about the previous night's Twinkie Incident.

To make her feel better, Paul told Malorie about all the many varied things Pedro had eaten.

"You look away for one minute, and they're in it," Paul said. "Last Thanksgiving, Pedro hauled the turkey off the kitchen counter. I had to serve it with no drumsticks. I flipped it over so my mother wouldn't notice, but of course she did. That woman misses *nothing*."

"You still served the turkey?"

"My whole family was waiting in the dining room. Honestly, what would you have done?"

"I don't know, but I'm glad I have a tiny dog that can't reach the counter." She thought about how it must be nice to be Paul, with a big family waiting for a turkey, whatever the condition.

They were in the break room, and Paul was pouring himself a cup of coffee.

"Careful with that," Malorie teased.

"Don't worry. I'm not going to spill this one all over myself. I'm not a complete idiot." He jerked his hand toward his chest in a joking motion. Exactly two-fifths of the mug's contents splashed all over his sweater vest.

"Oh, Paul," Malorie said. "That's such a Paul thing for you to do."

"I know," he said glumly. "What can I do about it? I'm so... Paul."

"At least your hair looks great," she said. Penny had done a remarkable job on that aspect of the makeover. It was too bad the Penntastic crew's attempts at a wardrobe upgrade hadn't stuck.

Paul gave her a thumbs-up and left with a wet shirt and three-fifths of a mug of coffee.

* * *

As for Princess and her tummy troubles, she was less hungry than usual, but other than that, she seemed just fine.

Malorie had a solid day at work. She got everything on her list done, but she stayed an extra two hours anyway.

That way when she got home, she wouldn't have quite so many boring hours to kill before leaving to meet Sacha at the dog park.

* * *

Malorie stepped out of her apartment building at ten o'clock on Tuesday night.

She was surprised to find Sacha and Duke waiting in front of the building for her.

Sacha had gotten a haircut. His short black hair was even shorter, which accentuated his widow's peak, man-in-the-moon good looks, and icy-blue eyes.

"Fancy meeting you here," Malorie said.

Seeing Sacha and Duke in front of her building was a new development. Sacha usually arrived at the dog park coming from the opposite direction, so the idea of walking to the park together had never been brought up.

Malorie asked, "Were you doing errands in the area?"

"Yes. This is an errand." Sacha turned and walked around to the trunk of his car—the top was up, so she hadn't recognized his convertible right away—and popped it open. "I have something of yours."

"I think I got everything already," she said, thinking of the items she'd bought at the Pier over the weekend.

"Are you sure you aren't missing anything else?"

"Not that I can think of."

He pulled a dry-cleaning bag from the trunk and brought it over to her. "I believe you may be missing a wedding dress," he said.

She looked down, saw the beading through the clear plastic window, and immediately knew it was hers. *Her* wedding dress. From the wedding-that-didn't-happen.

Sacha asked, "Is there anything you want to tell me?"

Malorie stared at the dress in disbelief. This was like the time she'd first seen Duke and thought Princess was in two places at the same time. How could Sacha have her wedding dress when it was still up in her apartment, in her closet? No. In the oven. No. On the kitchen counter. Come to think of it, she hadn't seen it around since the morning of the painting day.

Malorie recovered from the shock quickly and said, "Oh. That old thing." She wrinkled her nose to convey disgust.

Sacha asked, "Aren't you wondering why I have your wedding dress?"

"It's not mine," she said. "I mean, it was in my apartment, but it's not mine."

It wasn't like Malorie to lie, but having to explain everything about the wedding-that-didn't-happen would have been unbearable. She'd rather be a liar than tell that particular truth.

"I'll tell you why I have it," he said. "It is what people would call a funny story."

She wrinkled her nose and shrugged as if to say it didn't matter to her either way, since the wedding dress wasn't actually hers.

Sacha said, "The painting crew accidentally bundled it up with all of their plastic and canvas drop cloths. They didn't realize they'd stolen someone's dress until they were at the next job and unpacked it with the other stuff. That's when they called me. I picked it up earlier today from the paint store, then I kept it safe in my trunk for you."

"The painters should have thrown it in the trash," Malorie said with a hand wave. "Talk about a lot of fuss about nothing. I hope they didn't bother you at work."

Sacha tilted his head and stared at her, his icy-blue eyes seeing far more than she wanted to reveal.

"There's a garbage bin at the end of the block," he said. "I can throw it out now if you'd like."

She grabbed the bag and clutched it to her chest protectively. "I'd rather give it to charity," she said. "Someone should get some use out of it." She wrinkled her nose again. "This old thing." She tried to come up with more of a backstory, such as the name of the person the dress actually belonged to, but nothing came to her. She was not practiced at lying.

"Okay," Sacha said, with the finality of someone letting something go by his own choice. "Then I will wait here with the dogs while you take it up to your apartment. I assume you do not want to carry it on our walk to the dog park."

She didn't argue with him.

She ran back to the apartment and up the stairs instead of waiting for the elevator.

She opened the apartment door, hurled the dry-cleaning bag in blindly, then raced back down again, eager to put the whole sordid business behind her.

They walked to the park together, watched the dogs play for eighteen minutes, and then Sacha called for Duke. He walked back with her to the apartment to pick up his car.

The silence was almost unbearable.

Oh, they did talk—about the weather, the ice cream shop, the antics of Malorie's coworkers, and more—but they didn't talk about the dress.

For both of them, the silence about the dress was hard to take.

Malorie might have broken the ice by coming clean about the dress or by asking Sacha about the young woman he'd been seen with at the Quick Stop, but broaching either of those topics required a courage she didn't have in her. Not that night, anyway.

Sacha got into his car with Duke. He waved goodbye as he pulled away.

Malorie was discombobulated and unaware of her surroundings. She didn't notice that someone was sitting in the car that had been parked behind Sacha's.

That person was watching Malorie and Princess with great interest.

That person was hatching a scheme.

And Malorie had no idea what was in store for her.

Chapter 26

Lars Lundin and Yuki Noguchi

On Wednesday morning, Yuki Noguchi came out of the bathroom in her silky robe, arms crossed and face flushed. Her hair was still dry.

"You broke it," she said to Lars. "You broke my shower!"

Lars looked up from the pan of scrambled eggs he'd been frying and said, "That foreign thing was never installed properly in the first place. Whoever put it in did a lousy job."

"You are the most infuriating man I've ever met! You never accept responsibility for anything, do you?"

"I'm making breakfast," he said. "What more do you want?"

"I want you to pick up your dirty clothes. I want you to wash your shaving cream out of the sink when you're done shaving. And I want you to not break things that I specifically told you not to break!"

"Yukes," he said.

"Don't call me that."

"Yuki."

She crossed her arms harder. "This condo is too small for two people."

"It's a two-bedroom plus den. It's the same size or bigger than Malorie's apartment, and she never had a problem with my clothes or my shaving cream. Malorie had a shower that was installed properly and actually worked. Plus the hot-water tank was bigger. I barely get wet in your dumb shower before it goes cold."

"I want you out," she said.

"Yeah, yeah. I'm leaving for work in about fifteen minutes, and you can have your space."

"No. I want you out."

His jaw dropped. "Where am I supposed to go?"

"Somewhere else. Go back to Malorie. I don't know why you didn't marry her when you had a chance. She's a really nice person, and I feel awful about what happened. I've been avoiding her at work, and it's giving me an ulcer! I'm going to have to quit that job, Lars. And I loved that job. Why did you have to mess up my whole life?"

Lars slowly took the pan of scrambled eggs off the burner, clicked off the element, and walked over to Yuki.

"Come here," he said, holding out his arms. "Sounds like somebody woke up on the wrong side of the bed this morning."

Yuki wiped away a tear of frustration. "Everything's a mess."

"Now, now," Lars said. "Come to your big, strong Viking."

Yuki took three small steps forward and allowed herself to fall into his embrace. "You're a big, dumb Viking who breaks things," she said.

He held her and kissed the top of her silky head. "I know," he said. "Everything's a mess right now, and this condo is a little on the small side, but eventually, everything is going to be perfect. We're going to live in a nice, big house together."

She pulled away and looked up at him. "A big house? When?"

"After the wedding," he said. "I've got a bunch of money saved up for a down payment."

"After the wedding? But we're not even engaged."

"Not yet," he said. "But one day, we will be, and then, after the wedding, everything is going to be perfect."

"I hope so. I don't like how things are right now. My stomach hurts all the time." She hugged him again, which made her stomach feel slightly better. "We have to tell Malorie."

"I'll talk to Malorie," he said.

"When?"

"Soon," he promised.

"Today," she said. "You have to tell her today, or I'm throwing all your stuff out of the window. But don't tell her when we're at work. Tell her after work."

"Sure will, Yukes. I'll tell her today if it will make your stomach feel better." He kissed her head again. "Actually, today's not going to work. Busy day at the shop, and I'll be working past dinner. Tomorrow would be better."

Yuki pulled away, gave him the angry look he found so adorable, and then stomped off to get dressed for work.

Chapter 27

Malorie Meyers

On Wednesday, mid-morning, Malorie walked into the office break room earlier than her usual coffee break time.

Yuki Noguchi was already in there, making tea with green powder and a whisk.

"That smells good," Malorie said. "I've always wanted to try matcha. Can you add milk and sugar?"

"I'll make you one," Yuki said, turning her back to Malorie.

There was a gurgling sound in the break room. It reminded Malorie of the sound Princess had made after eating the Twinkie.

Malorie asked, "Are you okay, Yuki? I feel like we haven't even seen each other since I got back from my trip."

"Tummy troubles," Yuki said, her face still pointed at the cupboards. "How much sugar?"

"One cube. Two if it's bitter."

There were two plop sounds then more whisking.

Yuki finally turned around and handed Malorie the gray stoneware mug. "I hope you like it," she said. The mug was one of the two that Yuki had brought into work for her own personal use, because she couldn't drink out of a mug that had been made in a factory. Only mugs that had been hand-thrown on a wheel had the right "energy."

There was another stomach gurgle.

Yuki excused herself and left the kitchen without another word.

Paul came in, his head slightly turned as he watched Yuki walk away.

Paul asked Malorie, "Does she seem a bit off to you? I'm worried about her."

"Tummy troubles," Malorie said.

"Ulcers do run in her family," Paul said. He was the resident expert on the Noguchi family.

Malorie took a sip of the light-green beverage. It was terrible. She checked that Yuki was gone, dumped it down the sink, and poured a coffee in a fresh mug. As she was loading Yuki's gray stoneware mug in the dishwasher, Paul said, "Those can't go in the dishwasher. Yuki's mugs need to be handwashed."

"Paul, are you in love with Yuki because of her exacting standards or in spite of them?"

He looked down at his shoes. "She'd never be interested in a guy like me."

"Probably not," Malorie said.

Paul looked up, his eyes wide with surprise.

"You're a good guy," Malorie said. "You deserve someone who appreciates you. Forget about Yuki and get on with your life. The woman you meet eventually will be glad you did."

He blinked. "No one's ever put it like that. You may be right."

"And you need to find a better dog groomer," she said. "Pedro's fur is in his eyes again."

Paul said, "Thanks, Malorie. You're a good friend."

"I'm just a work buddy," she said.

"After Pedro, you're basically my best friend," Paul said. "I'm not ashamed to admit it. I live a very small life."

"You have a great life. You're one of the happiest people I know when you're not mooning over Yuki. And for what it's worth, I'm proud to be your friend."

Paul held up both hands in front of himself awkwardly. "Should we hug or something?"

"Why not?"

Malorie gave him a hug. She was surprised by how nice it was to be hugged by Paul, her friend.

The argyle sweater vest really enhanced Paul's hug value.

Chapter 28

On Wednesday night, Sacha was already waiting at the dog park when Malorie arrived with Princess. He was dressed in dark colors, and his usually serious face looked downright somber.

"Am I late?" Malorie asked.

"Now is okay," Sacha said. "We can talk now."

Malorie didn't like the chill in his voice. She took off her Chihuahua's leash and sent the dog to join Duke.

Sacha turned and watched the dogs playing. "Duke will miss his friend," he said.

"What's going on? Are you heading out of town?"

"I am already out of town," Sacha said, not looking at her. "This city is not my home."

"Then... are you heading home?"

"Eventually. I am doing some travel for business."

"But you'll come back, right? Someone's got to keep those kids at Butter Spoons on their toes."

"The shop is closed," Sacha said. "I closed it today."

"Why? I thought it was going so well. You had lineups every day."

"It was always only temporary," he said. "It's what people call a pop-up shop. It was only for a while. For market research."

"For market research," she said. Had their friendship also been a pop-up? For market research?

Sacha called for Duke.

The dog came but gave his owner a quizzical look as if to say *Leaving already?*

"I apologize for leaving early," Sacha said to Malorie as he fastened the dog's leash. "I have some business to attend to."

Malorie stared at Sacha, her mouth slightly open. Was this it?

He looked at her. "Yes? Something you want to say?"

There were a lot of things she felt, but it was hard to say them, so she said, "Maybe tomorrow night we can do something special."

"Special? Such as what?"

She looked around the darkened dog park and came up with nothing. Nothing that was appropriate for two people who were only friends.

"Do not worry about it," Sacha said. "I fly out tomorrow. I will not be here tomorrow night. We can do something special another time. Perhaps when I am back in town."

"When will that be?"

He looked down at his dark, somber shoes, and held out both hands. "It is late, and I do not recall the exact dates."

Malorie clenched her jaw as she lifted her chin. "Well, you have my number," she said, trying to sound friendly but her words coming out terse anyway. "And you know where I live."

He looked straight at her, his icy-blue eyes pale and colorless under the streetlight. "Thank you for making me have fun while I was here. People tell me I work too hard, but most people don't like their jobs."

"I love my job," she said.

"That is good." He tugged on Duke's leash, and then he was gone. He was walking away.

Malorie replayed the last words she'd said to Sacha: *I love my job.*

What kind of a goodbye was that?

Princess lost interest in the park and came to stand by Malorie. She rested her front paws on Malorie's shoe.

"I guess that's it," Malorie said. "I'm sorry, Princess, but your friend Duke has to go away for a while."

Princess tilted her head, making one ear flop.

"I don't know if he'll ever be back," Malorie said. "Tonight might be the last time you'll ever see him. Take a good look while you can."

Malorie couldn't make herself look at the man and dog walking away.

Princess stared up at her human and trembled, even though it wasn't cold that night.

"I'm just being honest," Malorie said. "It's not healthy to delude yourself. You'll find another—" Her voice pinched off, choked by the thick feeling at the back of her throat.

A couple with a Pomeranian arrived at the dog park and waved happily at Malorie. They had met the night of the Twinkie Incident. The couple's Pomeranian had also eaten a number of things that were bad for dogs. They were friendly people, new to the neighborhood, but Malorie didn't have any interest in chatting.

Princess, who had gotten along well with the Pomeranian in the past, showed no interest in playing with the dog.

She dropped her head, then tugged on the leash and pulled Malorie toward home.

Chapter 29

Malorie and Princess didn't go straight home that night.

When they reached the Quick Stop, Princess proudly led the way inside like she was a VIP at the place.

Justine checked the time, then said to Malorie, "You're here early. Did the crazy Russian stand you up for your usual dog-walk date?"

"Not exactly," Malorie said, and she relayed what had happened. It took twice as long for her to tell the story as the events had taken in real life.

During the time she discussed every word Sacha had said and what the subtext might be, she did not notice Princess slipping away. Neither Malorie nor Justine saw Princess grabbing not one, not two, but three Twinkies and then taking them around the corner to silently sneak-eat.

Justine did her best to cheer up Malorie, but Justine had also had a bad day, and neither of them was feeling cheered up despite valiant efforts.

When some other customers came into the Quick Stop, Malorie announced it was time to leave. Justine said she had some restocking to do, anyway. "Tomorrow will be better," Justine said. "I promise."

"The best thing about tomorrow is it won't be today anymore," Malorie joked.

Justine offered Malorie a high-five, which was returned.

Princess returned to an obedient Good Girl spot at her master's feet. There were no tell-tale gurgles coming from the dog this time, even though she had consumed three Twinkies as well as one plastic wrapper.

Justine said, "I'm off for a couple days, but I'll see you on the weekend."

Malorie wished her a nice time on her days off. "Good luck with your mean old landlord," she said. The landlord, who was nothing like Malorie's, had been a key player in Justine's bad day. "If he doesn't come around, I'll ask Doug about openings in my building."

"Thanks," Justine said. "You're a good friend. The crazy Russian doesn't know what he's missing."

"That's right," Malorie said with an emphatic nod. "Forget about him."

Malorie left the Quick Stop, telling herself she would forget all about the crazy Russian.

She did nothing *but* think about the crazy Russian all the way home.

Malorie didn't notice that someone with a hoodie pulled up over their head was following her or that the same person grabbed the front door to the apartment building before it clicked shut and followed her in.

Princess noticed and pulled on the leash, but Malorie chalked that up to the dog realizing she'd been shortchanged on her dog park time.

Malorie got to her apartment, opened the door, and spotted the wedding dress. It was draped over the back of a chair, where she'd thrown it the night before.

"No," she said to the dress.

Princess trembled, thinking she was being scolded for something. The human knew about the Delicious Things! Princess had been so quiet, so careful, but now there would be trouble! Princess would be called a Bad Dog!

"Not you," Malorie said to the dog. "I'm mad at the dress."

Princess cocked her head.

The human said, "This whole thing with Sacha leaving town is all because of that disgusting dress. I should have said something to him last night, when he brought it to me. Why did I have to lie? I'm such an idiot."

Princess jumped up on the couch and waited for the human to join her for some TV time before bed. Angry self-talk could wait. It could always wait. Princess lived her life with no regrets. Sure, her belly didn't feel entirely right with the Twinkies inside, but even so, she had no regrets.

"You stay right there," Malorie said to the dog. "I have to do something I should have done last week." She picked up the zippered bag with the dress and folded it for easier carrying. Then she folded it one more time, to crush it. "I'm going to find one of those clothing donation boxes, and I'm going to cram this thing in there. I just hope that whoever gets it next can avoid the curse that obviously comes with it."

Princess tilted her head. What was the human going on about? This wasn't part of the routine.

The human grabbed her purse, the keys—the ones for the car! They were going to ride in the car!—and left the apartment.

Princess jumped off the couch and went to the door. She barked once to let the human know that the human had left without her. How much fun could a car ride be without Princess?

The human didn't come back.

Princess barked a second time, just in case anyone was listening and wanted to feel sorry for the dog who had been left all alone while the human went out with the car keys to ride in the car.

Then, because Princess was a good dog, she didn't bark again.

She got back on the couch and settled down where she could watch the door.

A few minutes later, there was a funny scratching sound at the door. It was like a key being turned in a lock but not as neat and tidy.

The scratching went on for a while, and then the door opened.

Princess jumped up and barked once in surprise.

The person who came in the door was not the human she had been with for the past ten days.

It was another human. One that Princess recognized immediately, by smell.

The person picked up Princess and then, without so much as a single face-lick greeting, put Princess in a plastic box. A metal door closed, trapping her.

Princess didn't like that. She began to feel really terrible. It was hard to say if the bad feeling was due to being put inside the plastic box without any kisses or from the rumbling in her belly. The three Twinkies did not agree with being inside Princess.

Princess hunched inside the plastic box, trying to keep the Twinkies inside her. She watched as the human left a note for the apartment's owner explaining what was happening.

The human signed her name to the note, large enough for Princess to see the big, curving letters, even though she couldn't read. The name was Sharise.

Chapter 30

It took Malorie some effort to locate a clothing donation bin.

The one she'd passed by countless times, in front of the post office, had been moved.

Malorie couldn't help but feel that the removal of the donation box was somehow personal, somehow related to the dress itself and the curse it obviously held.

This was a sign, she thought. Not that she should keep the dress but that she had to try harder to get rid of it. She was being tested.

Malorie used her phone to locate other donation bins around the city.

The next-nearest one had also been removed.

Malorie stared at the empty metal pegs in the sidewalk in disbelief. She considered dropping the dress right there, but she feared the dress would find its way back to her if she did.

Sidenote: It would have. Her address was written on the dry-cleaning bag.

Malorie returned to her car and tried a third donation bin, this one associated with a different charitable organization.

The box was there, gleaming and yellow and welcoming.

Malorie placed the dress in the drawer and paused. She should say a few words. None came to her.

She pushed the drawer, and the dress dropped inside the box with a soft thud.

The words finally came to her. "Bad dress!"

She went back to her car and drove home.

Malorie Meyers returned to her apartment building exactly thirty minutes after having left. She felt exactly one hundred and eighty-eight pounds lighter. Lars Lundin weighed one hundred and eighty-eight pounds—he was tall, with very low body fat. Now that the cursed dress was gone, Malorie felt free of Lars for the very first time.

Why it had taken so long was anyone's guess. A wiser woman might have taken the fact the guy didn't show up for his wedding as a pretty big sign Lars *just wasn't that into* Malorie.

It had taken Malorie nearly another full month, but she had put the dress in the yellow donation bin, and therefore she was wiser now.

Malorie parked in her usual parking spot. She was still upset about Sacha's cold departure earlier that evening, but when she opened the lobby door for her apartment building, she felt light and free. Anything was possible. The future was wide open.

She was surprised to find Doug, the landlord, standing in the lobby. The older Scottish man was wearing a sweatshirt with a pair of flannel pajama bottoms, and slippers. Doug lived in the building on the third floor, same as Malorie, in a corner unit on the opposite side.

Before she could greet him, Doug said, all in one rushed breath, "Thank-God-you're-all-right."

"Why wouldn't I be? What's going on?" Malorie covered her mouth. "Oh, no. Has Princess been barking? It won't happen again, I swear. She's usually with me." Malorie used the hand that had been covering her mouth to smack her forehead. "Why didn't I take her with me?"

"You left the dog in the apartment?"

"It won't happen again," Malorie said. "Did she wake up the whole building?"

"The dog didn't bark," Doug said. "Not that I'm aware of."

"Then what's going on?"

Doug, his face waxy and his posture stiff, said, "There was a break-in."

That was when Malorie realized Doug was holding a golf club.

She knew, without being told, that the break-in had involved her apartment.

She ran for the stairwell. Doug followed and ran up behind her, puffing as he said, "We should wait for the police before you go in. For safety."

When they reached the third floor, Malorie took the golf club from her landlord and said, "I've got my safety right here." Then she charged into her apartment.

The first thing Malorie saw when she opened the door was her laptop. It was sitting out in plain sight, on the coffee table. What kind of a thief didn't take a brand-new laptop?

Doug was talking rapidly, explaining what had happened. Another neighbor had spotted someone using lock-picking tools on the door—Malorie's door. The neighbor, a tiny woman named Peggy, had been too scared to confront the thief, so she had called Doug, who'd been asleep. By the time the landlord got over to Malorie's apartment, the deed had been done and the perp was gone.

"I checked the whole apartment," Doug said. "Then I went downstairs to see if you were out walking the dog, and that's when you walked in. It just happened." Doug looked around. "Where's the dog?"

"I didn't bring her with me," Malorie said. "Maybe she's in Peggy's apartment."

"She's not. We thought you had her."

It was very clear that the dog was gone, but Malorie preferred denial to despair. She asked, "Is she not here?" Malorie called and whistled for the dog. There was no response.

Doug looked down and shook his head. "I think whoever broke in must have taken the dog." He glanced around. "They didn't take much else that I can tell. I guess your friend Sharise didn't want a brand-new laptop."

Malorie dropped the golf club. "Did you say Sharise?"

Doug pointed at something behind Malorie. "That's what the note says."

Malorie turned around very slowly. Scrawled across her freshly-painted wall, written in red lipstick, was a note. It read: *How do you like that, MALORIE? XOXOX Sharise*

Malorie collapsed against Doug in shock. Princess, her dear little dog of only two weeks, but to whom she'd become deeply attached, was gone.

Doug got out his phone to call the police.

"Don't call," Malorie said, recovering as the growing rage kicked her into action. "They'll only slow us down. We're going to get Princess back ourselves."

"We?" Doug retrieved the golf club from the floor and held it behind his back, away from Malorie. "I can fix almost anything with the right tools, but I don't know how well I'd fare against a woman named Sharise who steals dogs and writes on walls with lipstick. This situation has all the red flags a man my age has learned to be wary of."

Another person appeared in the apartment doorway, breathing heavily.

It was Lars Lundin, in all his long-legged, strong-muscled, heroic-jawed, fair-haired Swedish beauty. Malorie forgot all about dumping the wedding dress along with one hundred and eighty-eight pounds of

Lars. He was there. Her favorite person. Her closest friend. Her companion for the last fourteen years. Just seeing him in person made her face hurt even as the rest of her body went numb.

"Peggy called me," Lars said. "Someone broke into the apartment?" He glanced around, taking in the lipstick note on the wall and frowning. "Who's Sharise?" Without waiting for an answer, he said, "I should have been here. I'm so sorry, Babes. Are you okay?"

Malorie made a helpless whimper then said, "Someone stole my dog."

"The Chihuahua?"

Malorie didn't think to ask how it was that Lars knew she had a Chihuahua. He knew because Yuki had told him, but Malorie wasn't exactly thinking about who might have known what about her pets and when.

Weakly, Malorie said, "Her name is Princess. I didn't name her."

"Babes, c'mere," he said, holding out his arms.

Malorie went to his arms and let herself be held. She'd been reassured somewhat by having Doug at her side, and the golf club, but having Lars was a thousand times better.

"We're going to get your dog back," Lars said. "Don't you worry, Babes. People don't mess with me and my girl."

"Your girl?" She pulled back and looked up at him, her eyes bleary.

Doug, who was still standing there with the golf club, cleared his throat. "Good to see you again, Lars."

The men shook hands.

"Don't worry about any of this," Lars said, taking charge as usual. "I'll get Malorie's dog back." He grinned, turning on the charm and the dimples. "I guess she's my dog, too."

Doug took in the information coolly. "You're back for good?"

"For good, for bad, and everything in between," Lars said, using the well-worn phrase.

Doug walked over to the door and examined the handle. "If it's all the same to both of you, I'm going to change out this lock right now. For security."

"You're the man," Lars said.

"No. You are," Doug said. "I'm glad you came to your senses, young man." He nodded at Malorie, then excused himself to go get his tools and a replacement lock.

Chapter 31

A thunderstorm was rolling in as Malorie banged on a motel-room door, yelling, "Give me back my dog!"

Lighting strobed the dark sky, and the sky rumbled with fury. Rain started with a light patter that got progressively heavier.

This was the right place. Malorie could hear Princess inside the motel room, barking, which only made Malorie more determined to get through the door. Or the window. She would get back in the car and batter her way through the wall if she had to.

She banged one more time. The door didn't open. People in the other rooms were starting to poke their heads out to see what was happening.

"Do it," Malorie said to her accomplice, her voice as dead and cold as an action movie heroine right before the big battle. "I authorize you to use whatever force you deem necessary to get me back my dog."

Malorie hadn't imagined herself ever being involved in this sort of a scenario, but from the moment she'd seen that lipstick note on her wall, she'd known that a big conflict with Sharise Peterson would be inevitable.

It was three o'clock in the morning, and it was all going down right now.

What, exactly?

Well, let's roll it back a bit and see how Malorie got to this particular motel room door.

Back at the apartment, moments after the return of heroic Lars, Malorie grabbed some paper towels from the kitchen and started rubbing the lipstick Sharise had left on the wall. One detail in particular had to be rubbed out. Sharise had dotted the I in her name with a kiss. What a devil woman.

Lars said, "Babes, you're just smearing it around. That paper towel isn't going to do anything."

"It will come off if I rub it hard enough!"

"You need something to break down the oils."

Malorie stifled a sob. "I just had this wall painted!"

Lars came over, took the paper towel from her hand, and hugged her again. The landlord was still there, changing the lock on the door, but Malorie let out one long, embarrassing sob anyway. With her face to Lars's neck, she smelled his skin, and for an instant, it was all she needed. She breathed in that familiar, uniquely Lars scent that had been an integral part of her life for fourteen years, and she took comfort in it.

With his voice calm and soothing, he asked, "Who is Sharise?"

"Her name is Sharise Peterson. She's a woman who... used to work at the Half-Moon Bed and Breakfast. That place you booked for us. When I was down there, I adopted a rescue Chihuahua. It didn't belong to Sharise, but she thinks it does, so I guess that's why she came here." Malorie looked up into Lars's eyes, hoping he didn't poke too many holes in her story. "She's mentally unbalanced," Malorie said. "Obviously."

"Obviously," Lars agreed. "But she doesn't live here?"

Malorie shook her head.

"We could call the police," he said.

Malorie wrinkled her nose. "I don't have any paperwork to prove the dog is mine."

"Don't worry, Babes. Lars is on the case. I'm excellent at solving problems. It's what I do. First of all, we're going to call the hotels and motels in the area that allow dogs. We'll find this Sharise woman, and we'll get the dog back."

"But they can't tell you the names of their guests, can they? That would break all sorts of privacy rules."

Lars grinned. "I'll think of something."

And, to his credit, he did.

He called every motel and hotel that accepted pets. He lied and said that he was staying at that hotel, and he could swear he heard a Chihuahua barking down the hall. Depending on the personality of the person answering the phone, he used a combination of charm and entitled threats to get what he wanted.

When Lars was using his talents, it really was a remarkable thing to see.

He ended his most successful call with a grin. When was Lars *not* grinning? "Found her," he said. "Sharise Peterson." He wrote an address on a scrap of paper. "She's staying at a place by the airport."

"Alone?" Malorie didn't say it, but she feared Shawn Gunderson might be there as well. What if he'd gotten back together with Sharise, and she had turned him to the dark side?

"Single occupancy," Lars said. "It will be two against one. Those are good odds, even against someone who's mentally unbalanced like this woman clearly is."

"Don't be too hard on Sharise," Malorie said.

Lars raised one gorgeous eyebrow.

Malorie growled. "Let's get her and make her sorry."

"Should we take my car or yours, Babes?"

Doug, who'd been changing the lock on the door cleared his throat. "I'm all done here," he said.

Lars said, "What do you say, Doug? Want to come with us and make it three against one?"

Doug laughed and waved a hand. "If anyone asks, I wasn't here, and I didn't hear what I just did."

"You're a good man," Lars said.

"Here are the new keys," Doug said. He held them out in his palm. There were two keys.

Lars reached for one and pocketed it. "Thanks, man," he said to Doug.

Malorie took the other one and also thanked the landlord.

They locked up, went out to Lars's car, and drove to the motel.

Which brings us back to Malorie and Lars standing in the pouring rain, banging on a motel room door, demanding their dog back.

Malorie had authorized Lars to use whatever means necessary to get into the room, so Lars was now backing up, preparing to build up some speed. He was about to kick the door down when the door suddenly burst open.

Sharise was there, breathing heavily. The whites of her eyes were visible all around her eyes. Her posture wasn't that of someone about to do something active, such as throw a heavy chair onto a stage. Her shoulders were slumped and her head was dropped forward.

An aroma wafted out of the room. It was similar to the smell that emanated from the garbage bins at the dog park. No, it was exactly the same smell. Sharise had been wearing light-colored clothes. The clothes were now covered in dark splotches. Sharise was coated in dog excrement.

Sharise glared at Malorie and said, "I don't know what you did to this dog, but I don't want it anymore." Then she started crying. "I don't even know why I came here," she wailed.

Princess came running out of the room, her tail wagging. She was surprisingly clean, except for something that was—how to put this delicately?—trailing her closely. Lars used his shoe to separate the item from Princess.

"It's a Twinkie wrapper," Lars said. "Why is there a Twinkie wrapper coming out of your dog?"

Malorie suddenly understood what had happened. She'd seen it happen once before, but at least they had been out in the open, in a park, and it had only been one Twinkie's worth. For an instant, Malorie felt bad for Sharise, who'd had no idea what was in store for her when she committed the dognapping.

Malorie's pity feeling quickly passed.

Sharise stepped back into the room, still crying, and closed the door.

Princess came over to stand with her front feet on Malorie's shoe, waiting for the magical words.

"Good girl," Malorie said. "Princess is a Good Dog."

Princess smiled, and, in spite of the thunder and pouring rain, her smile lit up the whole universe.

Lars ruffled his soaking-wet blond hair and said, "Something tells me there's a lot more going on here than I will ever understand."

"Dogs," Malorie said with a shrug. "You turn your back for one minute, and they're eating the drumsticks off your Thanksgiving turkey."

Lars crouched down and rubbed the dog's chin. "Let's get you both home and throw you in a nice, warm bath. Maybe I'll get in, too."

"Oh, Lars. That tub isn't big enough for me, you, and your long legs."

"No, it's not, but I'd sure like to try."

Chapter 32

Malorie, Lars, and Princess returned to the apartment as the sun was rising.

"What a long day," Malorie said, stifling a yawn. "How about you and Princess take that bath together while I warm up the bed? There's dog shampoo next to the tub."

Lars opened the lobby door and held it for Malorie and the dog. "You're going to bed already? Why would you waste your time sleeping when you could be enjoying a reunion your big, strong Viking man?"

Malorie snorted. "Since when did you start calling yourself that? It sounds like one of Yuki Noguchi's silly nicknames."

Lars shrugged. "I've always called myself that, Babes."

She yawned. "Okay," she said, letting it go.

They got in the elevator and pushed the button for the third floor.

Then something unusual happened. Or, rather, didn't happen.

Every time in the past that Malorie and Lars had been in the elevator together, he had grabbed, poked, or pinched some part of her body. This time, he didn't.

While Lars was not prodding her, Malorie had a moment to think. She remembered the curious detail of Lars knowing that her dog was a Chihuahua. He must have picked that up from someone they had in common, yet Malorie hadn't seen any of their mutual friends lately.

By the time the elevator doors opened on the third floor, she knew how he'd known. She also had a good idea about where he'd been spending his nights.

They walked to the apartment door.

"Oh, darn," Malorie said, pretending to fumble in her pockets. "I must have left my new key inside. Hand me yours." She held out her hand.

Lars looked at Malorie in the hallway, asking for the key he'd just gotten from the landlord, and something in his eyes changed. It was as though a tiny light had been blown out.

Without saying a word, Lars handed her the key.

She unlocked the door, sent Princess inside, then closed the door again without going in.

She turned to face Lars, the key he had taken now securely in her palm.

"What's this?" Lars grinned. "A new game? Do I have to guess the password?"

"This isn't your apartment anymore," Malorie said. "When I signed the new lease agreement with Doug so that Princess was allowed, I had him take your name off. I thought it would be a good punishment for you when you came back, to have to sign everything all over again."

"I don't care that I'm not on the lease," he said. "Come on. Stop playing around. It's late. I got your dog back. What more do you want?"

She looked at him for a long time. She didn't know what she wanted, but she knew it wasn't Lars Lundin. Not anymore.

"Just go," Malorie said softly. "Go, before people start coming out of those other doors to go to their jobs. Go, and the people around here won't have to see you leaving me yet again."

"I don't understand," he said. "I got your dog back. Doesn't that count for something?"

"You need to set things right with Yuki," Malorie said.

Lars blinked rapidly and pretended to be very confused.

Malorie said, "She's not exactly my favorite person right now, but I can't say I blame her. You are a Class A con artist, Lars Lundin."

"I'm what?"

"Get out of here, and do right by Yuki. You're causing her stress, and she doesn't need it. Ulcers run in the Noguchi family."

"Oh, *that* Yuki." He laughed it off. "She doesn't mean anything to me. Sure, we've been hanging out, but I needed a place to stay for a while. That's all."

"And that's exactly what's wrong with you," Malorie said. "You look perfect. On paper, you're perfect. But in reality, you're just... a bad dog." She shook her finger at him. "Bad dog."

Lars was speechless.

Maybe he said something else, maybe he didn't. Whether Malorie actually got the last word that night or not didn't matter. She *felt like* she'd gotten the last word. It had felt even better than shoving the dress into the big yellow bin.

Malorie let herself into the apartment and closed the door. She immediately locked it.

Malorie walked to the master bedroom, which was filling with light as the sun rose.

Princess was already on the bed, warming up her favorite spot.

Malorie crashed next to the dog with one of her shoes still on and slept better than she had in months.

Chapter 33

Thursday

Malorie arrived at work shortly after lunchtime. She had already sent a text message to her boss to let her know she was running late. She'd promised to stay late to make up the time.

Penny had replied to say that it wasn't an issue. Malorie had more than enough overtime banked to make up for it. Penny was a great boss. It should have been easy for anyone running a successful company with dedicated staff to be a good boss, but Malorie had been around enough jobs to know that wasn't always the case.

Malorie walked by Paul's office on the way to her desk. She didn't stop in due to already being late, but she glanced in, waved, and made eye contact.

Paul gasped as he leaped up from his chair, spilling one quarter of a mug of coffee on his sweater vest. He didn't even seem to notice the spill as he made a bee-line for Malorie.

"Something has happened," he said excitedly.

Malorie didn't have enough information to react yet. "What did you hear?"

"Yuki quit this morning."

"She *what*?"

"She was crying in Penny's office, and then she left. Penny just sent out a memo. Yuki didn't even say goodbye."

"That's too bad," Malorie said evenly. "She was good at her job. It's a real shame when perfectly good arrangements fall apart."

Paul cast his eyes down. His cheeks reddened. "I stood outside the door for a bit, listening in," he said. "Just for a few minutes," he added quickly.

"Did you hear why Yuki was quitting? Was it because of her ulcer? Ulcers do run in the Noguchi family. I honestly wonder if drinking all that strong green tea is good for her."

"I don't know why she quit, specifically, but she kept talking about shame and dishonorable behavior." Paul looked at Malorie, his eyes sad and glistening. "Do you think she was stealing?"

"She might have stolen something," Malorie said. "But I wouldn't know for sure. I wasn't there. Maybe somebody else talked her into stealing something that wasn't hers."

"You think?"

Malorie shrugged. "Maybe it's a good thing, whatever happened." An idea suddenly came to Malorie in a flash. "I think I know someone who might be able to take over Yuki's job. My friend Justine went to school for industrial design. She's a little out of practice, due to life and kids, but she's got a great personality, and I know that's the main thing Penny looks for."

Paul gave Malorie a blank stare. "Yuki's not coming back?"

"No," Malorie said. "She's not coming back. And if I were her, I wouldn't, either." She waved for Paul to come with her, down the hallway. "Come on, Paul. Let's get you a dry shirt and a fresh cup of coffee."

Chapter 34

Malorie went to the dog park at ten past ten. She looked for Sacha and Duke, but they didn't come. They hadn't been at the dog park Thursday night, either.

Malorie had Sacha's phone number, but she didn't send him a message. What would she even say? If they ever saw each other again, she would tell him in person. Hopefully by the time they met again, she would have it all worked out, and it wouldn't sound as stupid as it did in her head.

Princess walked around the dog park glumly, her head low. She missed Duke. Even her eyes looked sad. She looked exactly the way Malorie felt on the inside, right down to the occasional tremble.

Then the couple with the Pomeranian showed up. The dog, who resembled a teddy bear, was unleashed, and suddenly Princess was no longer sad. She was Best Friends Forever with the Pomeranian.

The couple introduced themselves as Bradley and Jody.

Jody asked, "Where's your husband and the other dog? I sure hope everything's all right."

"He's not my husband," Malorie said.

"That's too bad," Jody said, a twinkle in her brown eyes.

Bradley asked, "Is that guy really Russian? He didn't talk much, so I couldn't tell."

"He's Russian," she said. "The accent comes and goes as needed."

Bradley said, "It's too bad that ice cream shop of his didn't work out. I was startin' to like that place." He rubbed his belly.

Jody elbowed her husband. "It was a pop-up shop," she said. "It was never meant to last forever."

Jody looked to Malorie for corroboration. "Isn't that right? The owner was your friend, wasn't he?"

"He was my friend, and you're right," Malorie said. "The store was only set up for market research. It wasn't meant to last forever."

The three of them turned to watch the dogs playing.

The Pomeranian had a temper, but she was also quick to forgive. Princess no longer looked like a dog who was missing her friend.

Malorie, however, was still missing her friend Sacha.

But rather than pining over him, she put on a smile and asked Bradley and Jody about themselves.

The couple had recently moved to the area and were interested in discovering the best places.

"Have you been to the Pier?" Malorie asked.

Bradley wrinkled his nose. "Isn't that place just a tourist trap, full of overpriced stuff ya don't need?"

"Ooh," Jody said. "I love stuff I don't need."

"You have to visit the Pier," Malorie said. "I recommend going on a sunny Saturday, when it's busy and all the buskers are performing. I'm going tomorrow, to meet a friend from work. He's got a Labradoodle, so the dogs will keep each other company if we have to go into any shops."

"That sounds great," Jody said. "What time are you going? We'll bring Susan." Susan was their Pomeranian. Malorie found it odd that their dog had a person's name, but the Pomeranian did have a Susan type of energy.

Malorie told them the time and location she had planned for meeting up with Paul, and, just like that,

Malorie had all sorts of plans to kick off the weekend.

If she was going to sulk and mope around about being single, bored, and lonely, she would have to get it in early, before coffee.

Chapter 35

As they did every year, people in the city retrieved their winter sweaters from their zippered storage bags. Summer turned to fall.

At Penntastic, business continued as usual. The new pattern maker, Justine, was fitting in great and working hard. A little too hard. A few people hinted to Justine that she might dial it back, just a notch, so she didn't make the rest of them look bad. Justine apologized and told people that she'd been so bored working night shifts at a convenience store. She had a lot of pent-up productive energy to spend. But eventually, she learned how to ease her foot off the gas pedal on Friday afternoons, along with the rest of them.

Justine instantly bonded with Paul, the accountant, and the five of them—Paul, Pedro the Labradoodle, Justine, Malorie, and Princess—took all their coffee and lunch breaks together. They hung out on the weekends as well when Justine didn't have custody of her twins.

Justine assured Malorie that she was only interested in Paul as a friend, at least until everything with her divorce was final. Paul told Malorie that he *might* like Justine as more than a friend, but not until after he'd gotten over the heartbreak of Yuki's betrayal. Paul had learned, as had the rest of the office, about Yuki and Lars. It was the talk of the office for a few weeks, much to Malorie's horror, but once people had it out of their systems, they moved on to other gossip.

The new thing to talk about in the break room was Penny's growing baby bump. There was a friendly gambling pool running with bets on the birth date and the baby's weight.

Penny pretended to be embarrassed about the whole thing and all the attention that was showered on her growing baby bump, but it was obvious to everyone she loved it. The company launched a new line of maternity leggings and broke sales records.

Malorie was excited for Penny but also excited for herself, because soon, she would be taking on more design duties.

When winter came, with all of its gray skies and rain, Malorie bought Princess a rain slicker and quilted jackets to wear on walks. It snowed in the city but not a lot. Princess loved playing in the snow, which she'd never seen before.

When they got home from their adventures, Malorie would have to pull little icy snowballs out from between the Chihuahua's toes.

In addition to the company and socializing opportunities, another great benefit of owning a dog was the exercise. Malorie had never been big on going for walks, but Princess boosted her human's activity level.

Even as the days grew shorter and darker, Malorie felt more energetic and happy than she had in a long time.

Chapter 36

In December, Penny sent Malorie on a blind date with a man from her husband's office. His name was Chad, and he was "going through some stuff," according to Penny, but also "the sweetest guy you'll ever meet."

Malorie met Chad, and his sweetness was apparent immediately. The "stuff" he was going through—the recent breakup of a long-term relationship—felt very familiar.

"I've got a lot of paperwork waiting on my desk for Monday," Chad said. "Sometimes when I wake up on Saturday morning, and I've got a whole weekend of nothing ahead of me, the only thing that gets me through it is thinking about that big pile of mail."

They were at a bistro near the indoor ice-skating rink, where they were planning to go for a winter skate after eating lunch.

Malorie poked at the purple lettuce next to her grilled chicken. Why was some lettuce purple instead of green? It certainly didn't taste any better than the green stuff.

"I'm boring you," Chad said.

She looked up at him and apologized. "I was listening," she said. "What you said, about looking forward to your mail, I know exactly what you mean. Thinking about my shiny silver letter opener was the only thing that got me through my honeymoon."

Chad dropped the grilled cheese he'd been holding. "Your what? You're married?"

"Penny didn't tell you? I was supposed to get married in the spring, but my fiancé was more interested in my bridesmaid than he was in me, so *that* didn't happen. I went on our honeymoon, since the whole package was nonrefundable, and it was both the worst and the best time I'd ever had."

Chad leaned in.

Malorie said, "The bed-and-breakfast was magical, and it changed me. I adopted a rescue dog, then, when I got home, I started making an effort to meet new friends, and now I hardly think about my mail at all when I'm not at work."

Chad blinked at her, then started to smile. "Tell me more about this magical bed-and-breakfast," he said.

"Do you like Lana Langtree?"

He squeezed his eyes shut and shook with delight. "Who doesn't?" He leaned in and said, quietly, "I don't date women, by the way. Penny knows. She said this was just a friend date. She told you, right?" He fanned his face. "I'm such a loser, getting set up on a blind friend date."

"You're not a loser," Malorie said. "It can be hard making friends, especially if you were in a tight relationship for a long time and you love your job so much you're basically married to it."

"Good. I'm glad you're fine with it. Now, tell me everything about this honeymoon of yours."

She did. And because she could tell they were going to be friends, and therefore he'd find out everything eventually, she didn't leave out the juicy bits.

After they'd laughed for a solid hour, Chad and Malorie left the bistro and headed next door to the skating rink.

They were in line for their skate rental when Malorie spotted a familiar face at the other end of the lobby.

It was Sacha Mikhelson.

He was wearing an apron and handing out ice cream samples under a banner for Butter Spoons.

Sacha.

Mikhelson.

There.

At the skating rink.

Chapter 37

The instant Malorie Meyers saw Sacha Mikhelson across the lobby of the ice-skating rink, everything she had been planning to say to him left her head. The whole time she'd been planning those speeches, she never thought she'd actually have to say them. When Sacha had left the city two seasons ago, she didn't think she'd ever see him again.

Chad elbowed her. "What size skating boot do you want? They recommend going a full size or a size and a half down from your shoe size."

Malorie made a sound that was not a shoe size, let alone a word.

Chad said, "Don't worry. I used to work in shoe sales back in the day. I'll take a guess."

Malorie pointed at the Butter Spoons kiosk. "Ice cream," she said. "I have to get some, and it's over there."

"None for me, thanks," Chad said. "I'll get skates for both of us and meet you over there." He pointed to a bench where people were putting on skates.

Malorie grunted something in the affirmative then set off toward the ice cream kiosk.

Sacha didn't spot her in the crowd, but Malorie saw the dark-haired man in the apron, and it was definitely him. He was handing out samples of ice cream, which seemed like the opposite thing people would want in December while ice skating, but people were lining up.

Malorie joined the end of the line, which was very long. Malorie realized that she, like Sacha, also disliked lineups. She avoided Delilah's on the weekend for that reason. She would rather have no French toast than wait in line for it.

Malorie finally got to the front of the line just as Sacha traded off with someone else in a Butter Spoons apron.

"Wait," she said, but her voice was drowned out by the din of people around her.

The young man who'd taken over for Sacha thrust a sample-sized cup into Malorie's hand.

"I don't want this," she said.

"We're out of chocolate," the young man said.

Sacha had disappeared into the throng of people that were now lined up around the back of the kiosk.

Malorie dropped the sample cup on the counter and stamped her foot. "I demand to speak to your manager," she said, her voice rising until she was yelling. "I need to speak to the crazy Russian! Get him out here, or I'm going to be a very difficult customer!"

Someone touched Malorie's elbow. It was Sacha Mikhelson. He had seen her in line after all, and he'd snuck around to surprise her.

"That was very good," he said, laying on the Russian accent. "You have been practicing. You play entitled customer very well, Malorie."

When she heard her name spoken in Sacha's voice, in his accent, she could have fainted. It was the most wonderful sound she'd ever heard.

"Sacha!" She threw her arms around him. It was the first time they'd ever embraced. He was more solid than he looked.

He chuckled and disentangled himself, his hands firm on her shoulders as he pushed her away. "Not here," he said. "What will staff think of crazy Russian boss who gets hugs from pretty lady?"

He had a point. The kid at the counter was staring at them, mouth open. There was also the issue of the impatient, ice-cream-hungry people waiting to get to the front of the line.

"Oops," Malorie said. "We're holding up everybody from getting their ice cream."

"It is free samples," Sacha said in the thick accent. "People always have to line up for free, or they don't appreciate."

"True, but I don't want to be rude."

"Difficult customer is always rude." He pointed at her face. "It is role you were born to play."

"Oh, Sacha. I've missed your weird sense of humor so much." She excused herself and left the line, moving over to the side. Sacha followed.

Once they were away from the crowd, Sacha said, "Duke has missed seeing Princess."

"Enough about the dogs," she said. "You're in town, and you didn't call me. Shame on you, Sacha Mikhelson. You're not a very good friend."

He looked away. "I am not."

"But I can't say I blame you," she said. Suddenly, the speech came back to her. "Sacha, the wedding dress was mine. I was supposed to wear it for my spring wedding to a man named Lars Lundin. I dated him for fourteen years, and we were always on the verge of getting married. I called his bluff on the marriage, and he proved what kind of man he was, in front of all our friends. He left me there, at the church. I threw up all over my dress."

Sacha's mouth was firmly closed. He was listening.

"When I met you, it had only been a couple of weeks," Malorie said. "I was still deeply in denial. I thought Lars was going to come back. That's why I told you I wasn't single. But then, some stuff happened, and I finally came to my senses. I donated the dress to charity, and Lars doesn't have a key to my apartment anymore. It's over. It's been over for months. Since the day I last saw you." She took a breath and pushed back her shoulders. "And I've moved on. I've got so much more going on in my life now. I'm a million percent happier. The only thing that's missing is you."

"Me?"

"I miss our walks. And I miss our friendship."

Sacha nodded. His expression was solemn. "This man, he left you at the altar? He was a runaway groom?"

"You could say that."

Sacha laughed. Not just a chuckle but a big laugh.

Malorie's eyes stung with hot tears that threatened to erupt. "You're laughing at me?"

"I laugh at him. Lars. The idiot."

"Oh." Malorie's tears went away, back to where they'd come from. "I don't know how I feel about you laughing at the most humiliating moment of my life. Nobody's ever laughed about it before. Not to my face, anyway."

"You want me to make this face instead?" Sacha adopted a clown-like sad expression that didn't suit him at all.

"Well, no," she said. "I get lots of those looks, and I don't like those, either. I don't like people's pity."

"That is because you are not to be pitied," Sacha said. "It is good that this man did what he did. He made you strong. A tree that grows sheltered from wind is weak."

"You're *glad* Lars left me at the altar?"

"Aren't you?"

She'd never thought of it that way. "I guess I am," she said. "And I'm glad he cheated on me with Yuki Noguchi."

"Who?"

"Long story," Malorie said. "She was my coworker and my bridesmaid, and she slept with Lars." Malorie wrinkled her nose. "I guess that wasn't such a long story after all. One of my other friends, Paul, loves it when long stories aren't long. You should meet him."

"You have a friend named Paul?" Sacha pointed to Chad. Sweet Chad, who was sitting on a bench with Malorie's rented skates. Chad saw them looking his way and waved back happily. Sacha said, "That is Paul?"

"That's Chad," Malorie said. "A different friend."

"You have many friends," Sacha said.

Malorie felt more of the speech burbling up. "Sacha, I just wanted to tell you that I value honesty and integrity. I value it very highly. And I deeply regret lying to you about the wedding dress. After everything you did for me, it was terrible that I couldn't tell you the truth."

In his extra-thick accent, he said, "Perhaps you were not ready for me to laugh in face about idiot Lars."

"You may be on to something. Tragedy plus time equals comedy, but you do need some time."

An attractive, twenty-something woman in a Butter Spoons apron came up and interrupted the conversation. "Darling," she said to Sacha. "Who's your little friend?"

"This is Malorie," he said. "Malorie, this is Galina. Galina, Malorie."

Malorie shook Galina's hand. She noticed a lot of gleaming jewelry on Galina's hands. She also noticed that Galina pulled away from the handshake and then draped herself on Sacha's strong shoulder like it had been put there for her to lean on.

Galina turned to Sacha, pouting, and said, "I'm bored of handing out free ice cream to these people. Give me some money for the casino."

Sacha said sternly, "You have to work first. You work, you get paid, then you do what you want. Go to the casino. I don't care."

Malorie was practically speechless. She did manage to ask, her voice hopeful, "Sacha, is this your daughter?"

Galina tipped back her pretty head and roared with laughter. "Good one," she said to Malorie. To Sacha, she said, "I will work for one more hour, then I'm going to the casino." To Malorie, she said, in an exaggerated accent, "Never work for crazy Russian." She rolled her eyes then walked away.

Sacha said, "You cannot hire good help these days."

Malorie took a step back. "I should probably let you get back to work. Thanks, anyway, for talking to me. It felt good to get that speech out of my head."

"Will I see you tonight?" His icy-blue eyes sparkled. "At the dog park? Ten past ten?"

Slowly, hesitantly, Malorie said, "That is the time I'm usually there."

"Good," he said. He waved again at Chad, who was still on the bench, then turned and walked away.

Chapter 38

Saturday Night

When Malorie Meyers stepped out of the apartment building, she was already too warm in all her layers. The weather was milder than usual for the middle of December. The snow that had fallen in November was gone, melted away. The sky was overcast and starless, with the clouds keeping the day's warmth in.

Malorie was momentarily surprised to find that her usually quiet park was overrun with people. Then she remembered it was the evening of the Mid-Winter Baker Street Festival.

The park was lit with countless tiny white lights and holiday decorations. A group of late-night choir singers was standing on the gazebo, singing Christmas carols. Local businesses had tables set up for sales of snacks and hot beverages. The place was teeming with people, including many children who were up past their bedtimes, hyped up on candy canes and the idea of Santa Claus coming down the chimney the next week.

Sacha Mikhelson saw her before she saw him and approached with two steaming, fragrant cups of hot apple cider.

"You came," he said. "I worried you would be scared off by the crowds or by me, crazy Russian man."

"I don't scare that easily," she said.

He looked down at the dogs. Duke and Princess were acting as though they might remember each other or might not, depending on the smells. But first they had to smell every part of each other, tails wagging.

Sacha looked up and then around, eyes narrowed. "Where is Chad? Where is Paul?"

"I don't know," she said. "Probably at home, but they might be here. I think Chad lives in the neighborhood." She scanned the crowd but didn't see him.

Sacha said, "You don't know where your friend lives?"

"I only met him this morning," she said.

"What about Paul?"

"I've known Paul for years. He lives over by the bridge." She paused and looked at Sacha. "Why do you ask? Is the crazy Russian jealous?"

"Yes." In the thick accent, Sacha said, "Crazy Russian is idiot for not telling you he is in town. Of course pretty lady have other friends. Now, jealousy. Crazy Russian could not eat anything today." Sacha shrugged. "Is only fair. He is idiot. He should have called."

"Paul is my coworker, Sacha. We're not dating. He did ask me out once, because our boss put him up to it, but neither of us wanted that to happen."

"Okay." Sacha waved a hand. "That is Paul. As for Chad, I do not worry about. I saw Chad at skating rink. Chad has very good style."

"He does," Malorie agreed. She took a sip of the apple cider. It set off fireworks inside her mouth. She hadn't realized how nervous she'd been to talk to Sacha. Her mouth must have been very dry.

Sacha took a sip of his then held it away from his face. "Too sweet," he said. "Shall we walk the dogs now?"

"Sure, but I have to tell you something. Sacha, I like you as more than a friend. When I saw you with Galina today, I didn't know what to do. I went on the

Butter Spoons website, and I saw that her last name is Mikhelson, like yours.”

“She was a surprise,” Sacha said.

Malorie’s chest ached. Her eyes stung. “A surprise?”

“My parents thought they were done having children and then, surprise, Galina.”

“She’s your sister?”

“Of course she’s my sister. Did you think she was my girlfriend?”

“I thought maybe she was your wife.”

Sacha threw his head back and laughed. He didn’t laugh much, but when he did, it was loud and spectacular.

“Don’t tell Galina I said this, but I have much better taste in women,” Sacha said.

“You do?”

He tossed his cup of cider in the nearby trash can. He took Malorie’s and threw it in as well.

Then he closed the space between them, put one hand behind Malorie’s head and the other behind the small of her back, and kissed her.

Chapter 39

Monday

Malorie, Paul, and Justine were having their mid-morning coffee break.

"Baby clothes are complicated," Justine said with a sigh.

Paul and Malorie exchanged a look, then Malorie asked, "Is there something you want to tell us?"

Justine nearly choked on the coffee she was sipping. "No! Heavens, no! I love my boys, but two is enough." She shook her head. "Raising kids in the city is tough. I'd move to the suburbs if I could."

"Ew," Paul said.

Justine said, "I'm always getting flak from my uptight neighbors about everything. The boys put some decorations in the windows, and I got a letter that it was violating the look and feel of the facade."

"That's too bad," Paul said. "We need to get you a better place."

"In time," she said. "I've got my eyes open for the right opportunity."

"So, you were saying something about baby clothes?"

"Yes. For work," Justine said. "Penny has all these ideas, but it's a tall order. The patterns are not just smaller versions of adult patterns. Take it from me, a woman who survived twins, quick access is the most important thing. The visual line on a pair of leggings doesn't matter when you can't get it off your screaming kid in the middle of a public washroom."

"You'll figure out something," Paul said. "You always do."

"Penny has high expectations of me."

"Penny will have more perspective after the baby comes," Paul said. He glanced up at the betting pool chart on the wall. "Come on, lucky number nineteen." Paul had April nineteenth as his date. It was three days after Penny's due date.

They shared a good laugh, then Justine said to Malorie, "Enough work talk. How are things going with the crazy Russian?" Malorie had been on the phone with both Justine and Paul after Saturday's meetings with Sacha, so they were mostly up to date, but they hadn't talked on Sunday.

"Can you believe he made me work for him? Sunday afternoon. The crazy Russian had me handing out ice cream samples at the skating rink. For several hours. He's trying some new low-carb, coconut-based flavors."

Paul pouted. "And you didn't bring any in to work for us."

"Soon," Malorie promised. "Be patient, Paul. We've only been officially dating for about one and a half days." She gazed off into the distance dreamily. "But it's been a pretty great day and a half. After we handed out ice cream samples, he took me out to dinner, then we listened to some live music at a piano bar."

"Sounds like a genuine date," Justine said. "Things have definitely improved between you two since he tried to steal your dog."

"They really have," Malorie agreed.

"You're an inspiration," Paul said. "You give the rest of us single weirdos something to hope for."

Justine smacked Paul lightly on the arm. "Hey! Who are you calling a weirdo? Just because I sleep upside down in a cave doesn't mean I'm a weirdo."

The two of them laughed. Sleeping like a bat was apparently some sort of in-joke.

Malorie said, "I must have missed something good on Saturday when you guys were at the Pier and I was meeting Penny's friend Chad."

"It's a short story," Justine said. "We saw a bat under the bridge."

Paul laughed. "I was so scared."

"Then I pretended to be a vampire," Justine said. Malorie didn't get it.

"You had to be there," Paul said. "How was your friend-date with Chad, by the way?"

"Good," she said. "It's funny. After all the excitement with Sacha, meeting Chad feels like it happened weeks ago and not this weekend. He really is interesting once you get him warmed up. Are you guys okay with me inviting him to our next book club meeting?"

They both said it would be fine, as long as Bradley and Jody, who usually hosted their literary get-togethers, were fine with one more.

Paul got up with a groan, refilled his coffee, and left the break room.

Once the two women were alone, Justine leaned in and said, "Details. I need details about the kissing."

"There was plenty of that," Malorie said, blushing at the memory.

"And what else?"

"He called me Malishka," Malorie said, squirming in her chair.

Justine frowned. "He can't even get your name right?"

"It's Russian. It's like calling someone *baby*. It's a term of endearment."

"Malishka," Justine said. She got up suddenly. "That's it! That's what we can call the new line of babywear."

Malorie wasn't so sure how she felt about having her special name used for commercial purposes, but she did have to admit it was perfect.

Chapter 40

Christmas Day

December seemed warmer than ever to Malorie, even though the weather was fairly standard. Sacha was always heating things up, which was something, considering the guy sold ice cream.

Malorie was so relaxed, happy, and full from Christmas dinner that she nodded off in the passenger seat of Sacha's car.

It had been a wonderful day.

Sacha's younger sister, Galina, had made dinner at her house. Dinner had turned out well, in spite of the fact that Duke and Princess somehow managed to get up on the kitchen counter and steal the drumsticks off the turkey.

Galina had moved to the city a few years earlier, and it was at her place that Sacha stayed when he was in town. There had been plenty of talk of him getting his own place there, since the city would be a perfect home base for rolling out the new franchise. Plus it was where Malorie—*his Malishka*—lived.

Over dinner, Galina had printed out some real estate listings she felt would be perfect for her big brother. Galina worked as a real estate agent when she wasn't being roped into handing out ice cream samples.

After dinner, Sacha suggested that he, Malorie, and the dogs tour around the city to enjoy the Christmas decorations and check out some of the listings. They ended up driving around for two hours, checking out houses, tentatively talking about their future together, and discussing the merits of different neighborhoods.

Malorie woke up from her cozy nap when Princess jumped up and started licking her human's face. The car was stopped, and they were in front of Malorie's apartment building.

Malorie yawned and asked Sacha, "Was I asleep for long?"

"Not long," he said. "I wouldn't have known if not for the snoring."

"The what? I don't snore."

"Of course not," Sacha said. "It must have been the car engine. I'll take it in to get serviced."

He turned off the engine and stepped out to walk her to the door. He left Duke inside the car.

"You can bring Duke," she said as she stepped onto the sidewalk.

"It's only ten yards," he said. "He can stay where he is."

They reached the lobby door. Malorie said, "You still haven't been inside my apartment."

"I have not," he said.

"Would you like to come up now? You can bring Duke."

"I would like to, but I will not."

"Oh."

"Do not take offense," he said. "I am old-fashioned. Your apartment is for you. It is not for me."

"Are you saying you're too good for my building? It may be old, but it's very well run."

"That is not what I am saying." He leaned forward and rested his forehead on hers. There was intensity in his icy-blue eyes. His voice thick, he said, "I would like to come up, but I will not. I am in no rush."

"That's fair. We haven't even been dating two weeks. Sometimes I get ahead of myself."

"You are not the one running ahead. I am the one who asked you tonight to pick the house we will live in once we are married."

She was stunned. "What? I thought you were just asking me for my opinion as a person who's lived here a long time."

With his forehead still on hers, he said two words. "Which one?"

She knew immediately. "The yellow one."

"I will talk to Galina to arrange an inspection."

"And a viewing," Malorie said. "We should look around inside in case they've done something weird with the room arrangement."

"Everything inside can be fixed," he said. "But okay. I will ask for a viewing." He tilted his head up and kissed her forehead. "Anything for you, Malishka."

They said goodnight.

Even though their last kiss of the night was short and sweet, the memory of Sacha calling her his pet name kept Malorie warm all night. The idea of moving with him into the yellow house wasn't bad, either.

Chapter 41

The New Year

In January, Sacha bought the yellow house. The interior needed some updating, but Galina assured him it was the best neighborhood, with excellent parks and schools for her future nieces and nephews.

In February, Sacha proposed to Malorie with a ring Galina helped him pick out. Malorie pretended to be surprised, even though Galina, who couldn't keep a secret, had blabbed all about it.

In March, Malorie moved into the yellow house. The renovations were perfect, and the walls had been painted Passion Pastel #5.

Justine moved into Malorie's old apartment, which she had loved and coveted from the first time she'd come to visit. She put bunk beds in the small second bedroom for her twins, who lived with her part-time.

There weren't a lot of young kids or families living in the building, so the older tenants were worried about the noise from the twins, as was Doug. They all came around once they'd gotten to know the boys. The twins were noisy and boisterous and loud. Of course; they were ten and a half. But they were also playful and friendly and caring. Soon they knew everyone in the building, and had adopted all the retired folks as honorary aunts, uncles, and grandparents. Justine had to post a memo on the corkboard asking people to not feed the boys so many cookies.

In April, Malorie's boss had a gorgeous, healthy baby. It was born on the nineteenth, which meant Paul won the biggest prize in the staff's betting pool. Malorie won the second prize for guessing the weight. The baby was an adorable little girl. She was named Galina, because Penny loved the name of Sacha's kid sister. They called her Lina for short.

In May, Malorie's first wedding date passed. She barely noticed the day passing. Her *real* wedding was scheduled for July, and that was the only anniversary that mattered.

In June, Sacha gave Malorie a thoughtful and personal prewedding gift: tickets for them and all their friends to see Lana Langtree in concert. He'd even arranged for an extra-long limousine to pick everyone up.

But that wasn't the only surprise Sacha had arranged.

There was one more left.

Plus one more surprise that neither of them would have guessed in a million years.

Chapter 42

The Night of the Lana Langtree Concert

A champagne bottle was passed around the limousine, and everyone filled their glasses. The whole group was in a jubilant mood, heading to the concert while enjoying the summer weather through the large sunroof. It was their second bottle of champagne.

Sacha raised his glass. "A toast to Malorie and all her friends, who I am proud to also call my friends."

Chad cupped his hand around his mouth and said, "I'm easy! Anyone who owns an ice cream shop can be friends with me!"

Everyone laughed and chipped in with their own personal comments. They were all fond of Sacha and frequently begged him to do the "crazy Russian man" accent all the time.

While the group was debating opening a third bottle of champagne versus saving it for after the concert, the limousine turned off the main street. They rolled into the pick-up driveway for a hotel.

Malorie turned to Sascha. "What are we doing here?"

"We have one more pick-up," he said.

"I thought we had everyone. What are you up to?"

"It's a surprise." His icy-blue eyes twinkled.

"I can't imagine how you can possibly top yourself this time."

"You'll see." Sacha kissed her forehead then said to the rest of the group in the stretch limo, "Make room, friends. Make room for two more."

There was already plenty of room, but people reorganized themselves anyway.

Bradley and Jody, who were seated nearest Malorie, asked her who they were picking up.

"I don't know," Malorie said. "Honestly."

Justine, who was sitting across from Malorie, next to Paul, said, "Leave it to the crazy Russian to always keep us on our toes."

Paul didn't say anything, but he did spill some champagne on his sweater vest, which was such a Paul thing to do.

Sacha's little sister Galina was there, looking like she might burst from the effort of having to keep something secret.

Malorie rolled down the window and watched the doors of the hotel lobby.

The brass-framed doors opened. Two familiar-looking men in their sixties stepped out, spotted the limousine, and waved.

It was Albert and Bryan, the owners of the Half-Moon Bed and Breakfast. They were the two men who'd been so kind and friendly to her on her honeymoon. They were the ones who had convinced Malorie to try on Lana Langtree's concert dress and wig. That was the night everything had turned around for Malorie's romantic life.

And they were there! In her city! For the Lana Langtree concert!

Malorie squealed with excitement. She pushed open the limo door and tumbled out. She ran at the couple with her arms open wide.

They hugged her and said how happy they were that she was truly surprised.

When they pulled away, Albert said, "You look spectacular. Can you believe Bryan wanted to phone you and warn you we were coming? I told him he'd better not dare! Not after all the trouble your new fiancé went through to set this up."

Malorie turned to make eye contact with Sacha, who was still in the limousine, watching her from the seat. She blew him a kiss. He nodded and turned back to the group, explaining to their curious friends who the couple were and how Malorie knew them.

Bryan said to Malorie, "I heard that Lana Langtree will be performing a brand-new song tonight. Can you believe it? We're going to be part of music history."

Albert rolled his eyes, poked his thumb at Bryan, and said to Malorie, "*This one* thought we were getting too old to ever see Lana in concert again. Can you believe it? We're only sixty-three. I say sixty is the new forty."

"I'm so glad you both could make it. How's Bingo? How's the house?"

Bryan said, "Both are under the watchful eye of a dear family friend, so don't worry about a thing."

Albert, who'd been watching the activity inside the nearby limousine, said, "You sure have a lot of young, attractive friends, Malorie. I can't believe you told us you hardly knew anyone back home. What a fibber."

"A lot has changed in a year," she said. "Such as this." She showed them her engagement ring.

They all fussed over the ring for the appropriate amount of time, and then everyone got into the limousine. Introductions were made all around.

Malorie sat next to Sacha and looked up at him with adoration. He nodded and squeezed her hand.

The whole group got to the concert and found their seats.

The opening act was a duo who performed some classic hits, a couple of their own songs, and a slowed-down cover version of Lana Langtree's biggest song. Throughout it all, they teased the crowd about the new song Lana was going to perform that night, for the first time ever.

Then, suddenly, Lana was on stage in all her glory. She came on dressed as a Las Vegas showgirl in giant feathered wings. She started up, and she didn't stop.

The seemingly ageless woman performed hit after hit, rapidly changing costumes between songs and demonstrating an athleticism that most women half her age didn't have.

"Phew," she said, breathing hard into the microphone as she finally slowed down and took a stool, center stage. "If y'all don't mind, I'm going to slow things down for this next one. How do you folks feel about listening to a new song I've been workin' on?"

The crowd erupted with happiness.

Lana waved one bejeweled hand for everyone to calm down. "Now, don't go getting yourselves too worked up. I haven't quite worked out all the kinks."

The crowd cheered even louder.

A stagehand brought her an acoustic guitar.

Lana tilted her head to the guitar and made a few small adjustments.

She said into the microphone, "This one's kind of a long story. Do you like stories?"

The crowd went wild.

Down in the audience, Malorie grabbed Sacha's hand, squeezed it, and kissed his cheek. She noted that Albert was also holding Bryan's hand.

Lana strummed a few chords then hummed a melody very softly. The whole audience leaned forward in their seats, straining to hear.

"Oh, I do love that," Lana said, laughing. "I love it when everyone gets all quiet. That's how I know I have your attention, and, you know me, I do love attention."

There was a smattering of laughter in the audience.

Lana strummed another chord and began singing.

The new song was about a special dress. A wedding dress. In Lana's story, the bride who bought it never made it to her wedding day, but her family wanted someone to enjoy the beautiful gown, so they donated it to a charity shop. A week later, another woman bought it just because it was her size. That woman didn't have anyone in her life who loved her, let alone a man to marry.

The woman hung the dress in her closet. When she went to bed that night, she felt very foolish. She tried to forget about the dress, but the dress wouldn't forget about her.

The dress had its own dreams. It longed to be worn one day by a beautiful bride. That night, there was a gust of wind that opened the woman's closet. The moonlight from the window struck the dress, and the dressed wished upon the moonlight to have its dreams come true.

The next morning, the woman met the man she would marry.

As Lana finished the song, the crowd didn't even wait for her to finish before everyone was on their feet, roaring for more.

Lana waved for everyone to settle down again. She spoke softly into the microphone. "Folks, that song is based on a true story. I was here in town not long ago. At Christmastime, I was visiting some folks here. My son lives here with his family. I let him think I came just to see him, but the truth is I wanted to spend some time with a dear friend. She and I passed by a secondhand shop with a wedding dress in the window. I said to her, Darlene—her name is Darlene—that dress is your size. I know by looking at it. We need to go into that store and buy you that dress. It will bring you good luck."

The crowd reacted with some hoots and cheers before settling again.

"Darlene is a stubborn woman, and, wouldn't you know it, she would not buy that dress." The audience booed. "So I went in and I bought it for her." The audience cheered. "The next day, Darlene was at the grocery store and saw a gentleman reading one of those trash magazines that had a feature story about yours truly. Darlene told the man that she knew Lana Langtree personally, and nothing those rags ever said had a grain of truth in them, because they don't, but if he would let her in line in front of him, she'd tell him a true story about good ol' Lana Langtree."

Lana paused to drink some bottled water.

The anticipation in the audience was palpable.

"Oh, they're married now," Lana said casually.

She pointed to the large screen that hung above the stage. An image of a middle-aged couple on their wedding day flashed onto the monitor.

Darlene, the woman who'd inspired Lana Langtree's new song, was wearing Malorie's old dress.

And she looked spectacular.

"And that," Lana Langtree said, "is the power of a good dress. It can turn your life around."

Down in the audience, Sacha Mikhelson turned to his fiancée and asked, "Isn't that your dress?"

Malorie was confused. "How would you know what my dress looked like?"

"You don't think I left it in the dry-cleaning bag, do you?"

Malorie gasped. "You sneak!"

"Galina tried it on," he said. "She asked me if she could have it, if you didn't want it, but then..."

"Then I lied to you. Like a chicken."

"I'm glad you did," he said. "You made me wait six months. People always appreciate something more when they have to wait in line." He dazzled her with one of his rare full smiles.

"At least things worked out for Darlene," Malorie said. "Good for Darlene."

"Good for Darlene," he agreed.

Then, just when it seemed things couldn't get more perfect, Darlene and her husband came out on stage, wearing their wedding clothes, and confirmed that everything Lana Langtree had told them was absolutely true.

The right dress changed everything.

If you enjoyed this novel, you'll love Angie Pepper's other books set on Baker Street, featuring more great romantic comedy plus guest appearances by your favorite characters!

For a full list of titles, visit the author's website at
www.angelapepper.com

Thanks for reading!

www.ingramcontent.com/pod-product-compliance
Lightning Source LLC
Chambersburg PA
CBHW061305210726
48293CB00003B/1125